HIS DAUGHTER

"The good father tells me you are engaged to be married"

[Page 301

HIS DAUGHTER

BY
GOUVERNEUR MORRIS

WITH FRONTISPIECE BY
C. ALLAN GILBERT

WILDSIDE PRESS

www.wildsidepress.com

HIS DAUGHTER

HIS DAUGHTER

I

MRS. GRANDISON cast an eye upon the mountain of hand-luggage without which she and her daughter were unable to travel, and abandoned the conventions.

"Dorothy," she said, "I'm going to get hold of that young American and fasten to him like a leech. He's got a broad back and only one valise. Don't move from this spot."

She departed, bustling with energy and determination, and in five minutes returned with her victim.

But Frederick Dayton did not feel like a victim. He felt as if he had known Mrs. Grandison all his life and had always liked her. She was a direct, unaffected person, from whom emanated an effect of well-being and common sense.

"Dorothy," she said, "this is Mr. Dayton. I've explained to him *why* we had to discharge Ben Ali, and he's volunteered to help us get these things on the train."

"Wasn't that nice of you!" said Dorothy

Grandison, and a sudden twinkling in her eyes
was answered by a sudden twinkling in his. If
he had spoken the thought with which her appearance inspired him he would have said: "What
a pretty kid!"

Miss Dorothy was between fifteen and sixteen
years of age, but sufficiently cool and sophisti-
cated to have passed for twenty. Frederick Dayton was twenty-four, and although he had graduated from Harvard, distinguished himself in
post-graduate courses in botany and landscape-
gardening, and had all but completed a voyage
round the world, there remained to him a certain schoolboyishness of manner and vision. He
fought against these things, not realizing that
they were attractive qualities.

"The question is," said Mrs. Grandison, "what
are we going to do for Mr. Dayton in order to
show our gratitude?"

"I think we had better ask him to share our
compartment," said Dorothy, "and to make
himself at home in the lunch-basket."

"Gratitude can be overdone," said Dayton.

"What does he mean by that?" asked Mrs.
Grandison.

"He says he's afraid we don't allow smoking
in our compartment," said Dorothy.

His Daughter

"Well," said Mrs. Grandison, "if he must smoke I shouldn't wonder if I kept him company. I suppose you'll stop at Shepheard's?"

"I'd hate to go home and tell my friends that I'd stopped anywhere else," said Dorothy. "They say that if you sit long enough on the terrace at Shepheard's sooner or later you'll have seen everybody in the world that's worth seeing. But maybe you've often been to Cairo?"

"No," said Dayton, "I'm seeing everything for the first time. And there won't be a second for years and years. When I get home I've got to settle down to hard work."

Mrs. Grandison looked him over shrewdly.

"You have the professional head," she said, "rather than the business man's. Now tell me that I'm wrong."

"I've studied to be a landscape-gardener," said Dayton.

"Oh, mamma," said Dorothy, "*why* did you wear that hat?"

"What's the matter with. it?"

"Looks good to me," said Dayton.

"But it can't," said Dorothy. "It's got five kinds of flowers on it and no two of them bloom at the same season, I know. We too have a garden. Oh, mamma, do let's make Mr. Dayton

His Daughter

come and fix it for us. Let's make a contract with him right now, while he's still cheap."

"They are going to open the train," exclaimed Mrs. Grandison. "I can carry this and this and——"

"Please *don't*," said Dayton, "I'll have time to make several trips. *You* secure a compartment and defend it at all costs."

"I'll stay here and be rear-guard," said Dorothy, and she cast a defiant and belligerent glance up and down the platform.

"That kid ought not to be so troublesomely pretty," thought Dayton. "It's against the law."

And, a parcel tucked under each arm and two bags in each hand, he followed Mrs. Grandison to the door of the first-class compartment which she had succeeded in wrenching open.

"I'm infatuated with your mother," said Dayton. (He would have preferred to say: "I'm infatuated with you.") "She's so good-looking and such a good sport."

"You wouldn't think she was a day over thirty," said Dorothy, "if she didn't fall asleep in trains and other public places, especially right after luncheon."

6

His Daughter

The pair stole a mischievous glance toward Mrs. Grandison's corner of the compartment.

She slept extremely well. You might have thought that she had just laid down her book in order to look out of the window.

"You might be sisters," said Dayton.

"Sometimes my father pretends to get us mixed."

"Why didn't you bring him along?"

"He came as far as Hong Kong. Then he got a cable and had to go back. Wasn't it rotten luck? But he'll be in Paris waiting for us."

"Are there just you three?"

"I've got a brother at Yale. A great big nice brother. He's a junior."

"Will you be long in Paris?"

"I hope not. I'm just dying to get home. I've got two daisy ponies and I don't know how many wire-haired fox-terriers."

"I'm looking forward to Paris," said Dayton. "My sister married a Frenchman—De Séjour. They know everybody and entertain a lot, and so I'll see Paris from the inside."

"Wouldn't you hate to marry a foreigner?"

"My brother-in-law is a splendid man," said Dayton. "He's not a bit like the comic-paper

7

Frenchman. He's bigger than I am, and blonder."

"That's funny. I thought they were all small and dark."

"I used to think that. Then I went to school in Tours, and I found out that there are just as many kinds of Frenchmen as there are Americans."

"You must speak wonderful French."

"It's funny, but I don't. My sister and I had two years in Tours, and she came through speaking the loveliest French you ever listened to. But I didn't. I read it as easily as I do English, but when it comes to talking—why, I get the sexes all mixed up, and you'd know I was an American a mile off. I think languages come harder to men than to girls, don't you? Of course you speak French?"

"Oh, yes. I had a Breton *nounou*, and then a French governess."

"Say something. I'd like to hear your accent."

Without hesitation and in very pretty French she repeated some verses:

> "C'est chose bien commune .
> De soupirer pour une
> Blonde, châtaigne ou brune
> Maîtresse.
> Lorsque brune, châtaigne

8

His Daughter

Ou blonde, on l'a sans peine,
Moi, j'aime la lointaine
Princesse."

"But what a lovely poem!" he exclaimed.
"What is it? Tell me at once. Is it out of the
'Princesse Lointaine'?"

She nodded.

"I'll get it at once and read it. Do you know
'Cyrano' by heart, too?"

She nodded again, and said "Almost."

"I saw Coquelin do it," boasted Dayton.

"He must have been a wonder. I've only read
it and read it."

Then for a time they looked out of the windows
at the sand-hills and valleys of the desert, and
discovered resemblances between certain hills and
certain animals. That one looked like a yawning
lion; that was a camel lying down. But it must
be confessed that Dayton gave more attention to
Dorothy Grandison's profile than to the shapes
and colors of the sands.

She was so pretty and companionable and
American that he wished she was older. If she
had been two or three years older he would have
enjoyed starting a flirtation with her.

"I suppose you'll be coming out next winter?"
he said.

"Not till the year after. I'm not sixteen yet."

9

His Daughter

"*Really ?*"

"Not till next month."

"Somehow you seem older than that."

"Well, I've played a lot with older people. I suppose that's why."

"Will you have a ball or a tea, or a big theatre-party, or what ?"

"Why, I think it will be simplest just to begin going to things. But maybe I won't like parties. A few people are more fun than a lot. And I like being outdoors best. I'm crazy to begin riding again. I've only ridden twice since we started. Twice in California at Burlingame, and of course elephants in India, but they don't count."

"We must have some rides in Cairo."

"Oh, do you think we could ?"

"I'm sure of it."

"Are you good ?"

"Not very. It's like my French. I can stick on and sometimes get myself understood. The fact is, I'm an awful duffer at things."

"I don't believe it."

"Well," said Dayton, "live and learn."

"Are you a duffer at landscape-gardening, too ?" she asked, and at the same time smiled disarmingly.

"That," he said, "is what I've got to find out. It's my last hope."

His Daughter

"I like natural gardens," she said, "but I hate fountains, and lop-sided nymphs, and gravel."

"So do I," said Dayton, "and such things are very hard to draw."

"Of course you have to draw, don't you? I never thought of that."

"And I don't draw well," said Dayton. "I don't draw well enough. But I'll be in Paris all spring and summer and I'm going to work very, very hard."

"Draw something now."

"Now really!"

"I showed off my French for you, like a little man. Now you've got to show off for me."

So, on a leaf of his note-book, he drew, in spite of the wriggling and jerking of the train, a very creditable garden-gate with a long perspective of shrubs and flowers.

She said it was a beautiful garden and that it was wonderful of him to be able to draw like that, and then she came and sat by him and looked over his shoulder while she made him draw other things.

She was no longer a troublesomely pretty young lady, not quite old enough to be taken seriously; that sophistication acquired by travel and associating with older people vanished, and in a twinkling she became a child. To amuse a child of eight he would have drawn the same comical animals and told the same legends about them. In her eagerness to see and to laugh she leaned against his shoulder, and once her hair tickled his neck so that he gave a great shivery wriggle and spoiled a hippopotamus.

"How do you expect me to draw," he said, "with you flopping all over the place like that?"

"'Scuse," she said.

All in a crum of time they had become intimate, with the beautiful sexless intimacy of little children. Nor upon the present awakening of Mrs. Grandison did they lose that attitude toward each other.

As a matter of fact, Dayton himself was by no means grown up. At most times he could have been readily absorbed into any childish game such as old maid or twenty questions. And toward life itself he retained high and romantic ideals. Almost all of his school and college days had been passed in strict training and self-sacrifice. To play upon the "scrub" for four seasons and withstand the buffetings of the Varsity is a career little short of heroic. All his springs and early summers had been devoted to rowing. And it was not until his senior year that he was given a seat in the boat and won his "H" in a beaten

His Daughter

crew. There was a difference of opinion as to whether he should have been tackle on the Varsity or not. Some people felt that his really fine defensive play might have staved off the Yale attack and led to a Harvard victory. But he never had his chance. And the fact is of no great importance. It is important to remember that in many ways the boy who devotes himself to a college cause, which demands of him self-sacrifice and early hours, develops slowly. For Dayton to have posed as a man who knew his way about would have been sheer affectation. His body was far more seasoned than his mind, for it had formed habits. It craved exercise, work, and water as a drunkard craves alcohol. It loathed the idea of going soft and shapeless. It was a splendid, clean, pliant body in which no nerve twitched. The position in which he was when sleep came to him he retained the whole night through. If he had tried to stay awake all night he would have failed, just as a child would.

Though he had sometimes been noisy at noisy dinners attendant upon the breaking of training or the marriages of friends, he could not imagine himself taking a drink by himself and for the drink's sake. And concerning women he had much of the shyness and curiosity of innocence.

His Daughter

The attitude toward women of many of the men he had talked with during his trip round the world had opened his eyes to the fact that he himself was a youth of either extremely good morals or extremely cool temperament. And he often wondered which, oblivious of the fact that good morals are not an inheritance or an accident but an achievement. The man who even partially triumphs over great temptations has more moral force, perhaps, than the man who has never been tempted at all.

Such temptations as had from time to time presented themselves to Dayton he had resisted almost automatically. But this did not prove either that he was moral or sluggish. It proved only that the particular temptations had neither power to shake such moral strength as he did have nor to rouse in him any impulses which were in the least difficult to school. The man who for the sake of appearances refuses the last slice of bacon might very well under other circumstances fight his best friend for the carcass of a rat.

For men who did not resist their temptations he had the hearty contempt of extreme youth. In other words, he made no allowance for the strength of their particular temptations. But he had the sense and good manners to keep his contempts and his judgments to himself. Nor could he have been brought to pose as a particularly virtuous young man. . . .

"*Do* smoke," said Mrs. Grandison, waking up.

"Not now," exclaimed Dorothy. "He's drawing pictures. But of course if you really want to."

"I don't. As a smoker I've never been confirmed."

Dorothy giggled.

"Once when I was a little boy there was a terrible smoking scandal back of our barn. Up to that time I'd never smoked in my life. It was the other boys. But when my father asked me, I was ashamed to confess that I'd never smoked. Isn't that a funny idea? I suppose I thought it was an unmanly record, and I'm afraid I lied to him. Then the lie got on my nerves, and the only way I could think of to right it was to smoke. Aren't kids *great*? So I stole one of my father's cigars. . . ."

"And it made you ill?"

"I didn't like it, but it didn't make me ill. And then my aunt promised me a thousand dollars if I wouldn't smoke till I was twenty-one. And I didn't. But that was easy, because most of the time I was in training trying to get on the school teams and then the college teams."

"And of course you did."

His Daughter

"I made the crew at the last time of asking," said Dayton. "I just squeezed in. And we were beaten by Yale, and I suppose you are glad?"

"Of course I'm glad," said Dorothy. "Did you cry?"

"Yes," said Dayton, "we all cried and collapsed. The losing crew always has to. It's the rule. But the other fellows, who'd worked just as hard as we had, and who weren't a bit better conditioned, turned right round and rowed back up the river. Insulting, wasn't it? If we'd won we would have done the same thing to them."

Dorothy withdrew to a little distance and regarded Dayton critically. He looked very blond and strong and placid. It was difficult to picture him as distressed and unhappy.

"I can't imagine what you'd be like, crying," announced Dorothy. "I don't know whether it would be funny or horrid. Mamma, did you ever see a man cry?"

But Mrs. Grandison would not commit herself. Either she had never seen a man cry or did not wish to appear uninitiated in the eyes of the young people.

They had not been many days in Cairo before it dawned upon Dayton that he was filling Dorothy Grandison's mind to the exclusion of everything else. She was terribly "mashed" on him, as we Americans say of a passion which we do not wish to dignify by the name of love. And in every possible way she revealed her state of heart to him and to everybody else. Mrs. Grandison joked with him about his conquest, and besought him not to allow any chivalrous consideration for the child's infatuation to influence any of his comings or goings. But that infatuation of hers was very easily satisfied, since the mere fact of being his companion upon an excursion of some sort or other made her ecstatically happy. She loved the sun; she did not at this time wish that it could love her back. It was enough that it should shine upon her from the heavens, and that there should come between them no cloud. If she had been a little boy instead of a little girl she might have adored him in much the same way. Perhaps it would be more just to describe her as not in a state of love but of hero-worship. She imagined situations in which she laid down her life for him. Some of them, which had touches of true dramatic value, became very real to her, and she lived them over and over again.

Upon Dayton the affair had an outer and an inner effect. He managed outwardly to appear older, graver, and more experienced. But inwardly he lapsed from the middle twenties to

His Daughter

the late teens. He built very romantic edifices upon the foundation of her attachment. He took it seriously. It was not a mere schoolgirl mash, but love. It had about it a quality of permanency. Years might pass and find her still the same.

If she had only been a few years older! She would be just the kind of girl he would fall in love with if he ever did fall in love with anybody. She was keen, and pretty, and unspoiled, and wellborn. They had tastes in common. If only she had been born even two years earlier!

In his open attitude to her he was most circumspect and older-brotherly. Nobody could have guessed that in his secret heart the romance was a matter of real moment to him. Into that secret place he took her often—not as she was, but as she would be in a few years. His pleasantest imaginings had to be based upon that hypothesis, and this—that he was also in love with her. But the one hypothesis depended on the other. He couldn't be in love with a girl of sixteen, but with the same girl had she been eighteen he could not have helped being in love. And for no better reason than this—that the one thing was acceptably conventional and the other wasn't.

There were many white days; those in which

18

His Daughter

Dayton accompanied the Grandisons on some one of Cairo's thousand excursions. Each of them lived their experiences over and over again, but in different ways. Dorothy dwelt upon them in exact detail; revelling in memories of how her hero had looked and of what he had said; but Dayton relived them in imagination. In short, he raised the age of one of his companions and excluded the other. And then he had beautiful times.

Twice he dreamed about her. In each case she was older and loved him just as much as ever. In one dream they swung in a hammock. The ropes of the hammock were not attached to anything, and when they swung back—'way back and up—they looked down and could see, far below their feet, the full moon. But the other dream was not so pleasant. He was crying very bitterly about something or other, and she was standing at a window looking out and considering what she should do. It was a cold and cruel dream. Even the fact that he had a *café-au-lait* silk stocking tightly knotted about his head failed to touch it with humor.

One afternoon, having ridden camels up from the edge of the desert, they all three climbed the Great Pyramid of Cheops. But a fifth of

His Daughter

the way up Mrs. Grandison's legs began to give
out and she wisely decided to attempt no
more.

From the Arabs who accompanied them the
young people refused all offers of assistance. It
was a point of pride with them. They wanted
to tell their friends at home that they had sur-
mounted all the boasted difficulties of the ascent
without aid of any kind.

The way up the Great Pyramid, divided into
its component parts, is simplicity itself. A well-
practised Arab goes up as easily and regularly
as a housemaid goes up a flight of stairs.

And indeed the pyramid, stripped of its granite
facing, is nothing but four great flights of stairs
that narrow as they ascend. The individual
steps, however, do not follow the simple archi-
tectural formula of seven inches by ten; some
of them are ten inches broad and as high as a
table. Some are higher, and there are very few
which may be easily negotiated by legs of average
length and elasticity. And the upper muscles
of the thighs get a stretching which Nature did
not anticipate. Not less is the effect of the Great
Pyramid upon the spirit-levels of the inner ear.
No precipice, even from the height of a mile,

20

His Daughter

has the dizzying effect of those interminable ranks of steps, seen from above.

A third of the way up they rested a little and looked down, and already the effect of the height was troubling.

"I didn't think it was nearly so steep," said Dorothy.

"It *is* steep," said Dayton. "If you did fall, and didn't happen to catch on that broad step just below, you'd go the whole way."

"The more I look the more I want to try."

"Try what?"

"Try if you really would go the whole way."

"Then don't look," said Dayton firmly; "you're showing symptoms of precipicitis."

"Do your legs feel funny?"

"How do you mean—funny?"

"Very long and woggly, like that baby camel's we saw. Mine do."

"They ought to," said Dayton; "they've been pulled by all nations. But my heart's going some. It could drive a nail with one blow."

The climb had ceased to be amusing. It was hard work and hot work. Dayton, a little soft with travel, was drenched.

The Arabs had not turned a hair. They breathed like sleeping children and chatted in

His Daughter

Arabic, a language which Dayton and Dorothy Grandison had the good fortune not to understand. It would not have pleased them to hear that they were descended from pigs, and that the near sight of them was enough to make a blind camel sick at all of his many stomachs.

When at last they reached the twelve-foot-square platform which is the top of the pyramid, Dorothy flung herself face down and buried her face in her arms. Dayton too flung himself down and for a long time panted like a dog. And he smiled a little at the wonder of being so completely done up. He had fancied himself a strong man in the pink of condition, only to discover that he had certain muscles for which until that day he had never found any use.

He rose to his feet with great difficulty. The muscles of his thighs were so stretched that he could hardly control his legs. Thoughts of having to descend the pyramid disturbed him extremely. He walked to the edge of the platform, looked over, and turned away quickly.

By this time Dorothy had gathered herself into a sitting position. She was dead white, with a spot of vermilion in each cheek.

"Help me up," she said, "I want to see if I can stand." He had to support her.

His Daughter

"They used to have knee-joints and ankle-joints," she said; "now they are all joints like snakes."

"They've got nothing on mine," said Dayton. "Shall I tell you a secret?"

"Tell."

"I looked over the edge just now, and I've climbed mountains and looked over precipices and never minded a bit, but I tell you frankly that I backed away just as fast as I could. Want to look? I'll hold you."

He held her by the hand, and while she looked down the red, interminable broken slope, he looked up at the sky. It seemed ever so much nearer than the desert.

"We'll tell people how we climbed the pyramid boldly and without aid," he said, "but we won't tell them how we got down. Personally I'm going to shut my eyes tight and let two of those fellows do the rest."

But when it came to the point his pride rebelled. And in after-years he looked back on his unaided descent of the Great Pyramid as his one and only real triumph of mind over matter.

But they put off the descent a long time, until the sun had sunk so low that the shadow of

His Daughter

Cheops stretched across the whole valley of Egypt, like a river of darkness.

Dorothy Grandison was perfectly happy. She was with him. He might joke, he might tease her, he might be serious; whatever he did was perfect. Life was perfect; she was alive; and being alive it was delightful to imagine deaths which she died for him.

The mystery and wonder of Egypt did not touch her. But with Dayton it was different. By no means a churchgoing or ritualistic young man, the expanse of desert unrolled beneath his feet, and the silence, and the mystery of that monument on which they were resting gave him deep religious emotions. He no longer thought: "If she were only a little older what a jolly time we would be having!" He did not think about her at all.

"What are you thinking about?" she asked.

"I was thinking that the shadow of Cheops was old when the sun was young."

To Dorothy that seemed a wonderful and shivery thought.

"And I was thinking that thousands of people who have been dead for ages and ages have sat up here and thought the same thing, and that it didn't matter what they thought or when they died."

His Daughter

"If it didn't matter when people died," said Dorothy, "then it wouldn't matter what they did while they were alive, would it?"

They talked for some time in this childish strain and felt as if they were drawing very close to great truths.

"And yet," said Dayton, "what we do *must* matter."

After dinner he strolled round to the Sphinx bar with some casual acquaintances, and after some music and some Scotch whiskey they yielded to the seductions of a guide who would not take no for an answer, piled into a one-horse victoria, and were given some exceedingly intimate glimpses of night life in the native quarter.

But only Longstreet, the Englishman, appeared frankly and unaffectedly to enjoy the experience. The others, as the night grew old, became more and more solemn and depressed. To Longstreet the vice that was flaunted in their faces seemed neither vicious nor educational, only funny. And it seemed also funny to him that he, a clean-run, sleep-loving Englishman, should spend a whole night upon such sights. And so he was in high good humor and laughed at the slightest excuse.

Dayton envied Longstreet secretly. It was

impossible for him not to take Cairo's tenderloin very seriously indeed, and he resented this. Each den that he entered he entered with real reluctance, and yet he found it impossible to say, as he wished: "I've had enough of this; let's go home." For this weakness of will he tried to excuse himself and the others with: "Every man ought to see this sort of thing once, and know how the submerged live. No man can be a force for good unless he knows what he's got to fight against."

In an upper room, over a black, shaft-like courtyard that stank, musicians squatting on the floor made a dance-music to which perhaps Cleopatra had beaten time in her day, and when our sightseers—the solemn ones and the one that laughed—had been seated, an Arab girl came before them and danced.

She was very young. She was no older for an Arab than Dorothy Grandison was for an American. Dayton made this comparison in his mind, and at the same time felt that he was at fault even to have thought of that pretty and pure and friendly child in such surroundings.

But this Arab girl was not like other dancers they had seen in the quarter. The brownness of her skin was in itself a kind of garment, and

His Daughter

by the contemptuousness of her bearing and the sullen, defiant curve of her mouth she produced an extraordinary effect of modesty and self-respect.

Dayton found himself thinking: "There is a person who has touched pitch without being defiled."

Longstreet's laughing mood was over.

"That girl," he announced, in his clear English voice, "is beautiful."

And he spoke the truth. That defiant head and perfect body should have been perpetuated in bronze. Instead they would perish in disease and corruption. And yet, as she danced her slow rhythmic dance, sullen and contemptuous, she seemed to defy time and experience.

"There's eternal youth for you."

And in his heart Dayton echoed that thought and added: "Uncorrupted and incorruptible."

In their depths the girl's eyes smouldered with unawakened fires. If ever a man touched her heart, for that man she would endure torment and death. This was written very plainly in the depths of her eyes. As for all other men, let them come and go, look and desire, they were of no more account than dogs.

An immense pity for the girl arose in Dayton's

heart. But this was complicated by other feelings. He imagined what it would be like to have such a girl in love with him—not with Dayton the American landscape-gardener, but with Dayton if Dayton happened to be an entented, stallion-riding young Arab of her tribe. And he began to think that the night had been well spent. For she was making him feel more tenderly and more chivalrously toward all women, and more understandingly.

The Arab girl danced, and behind the bluish tribal mark low on her forehead her mind worked and received impressions.

Dayton's broad shoulders, his blondness, and the extreme purity of his skin were not lost upon her. She resented his expression of cool placidity and, with a view to disturbing it, danced more directly for him than for the others, and from time to time, through narrowed lids, looked enigmatically into his frank and not very deep blue eyes.

Each time she read in those eyes admiration, it is true, and friendliness and pity. So that gradually her own expression became less sullen and once she smiled at him—not as sirens smile but as children.

Longstreet's laughter was heard again.

His Daughter

"Dayton's made a conquest!" he exclaimed.

From beneath scowling brows the girl shot him a dagger look and Longstreet's laughter died in his mouth. The dance ended. The girl simply turned her back and walked out of the room.

But she came into the dark hall at the head of the stair just as they were leaving. She was clothed now in a one-piece dress of dark red, and there were clinky chains of semi-precious stones about her neck.

"She came to find if you gentlemen not like her dance," said the guide.

"Tell her we loved it," said Dayton. "It was splendid."

In that same tone he would have praised some one who had sung pleasingly an innocent song.

"Good-by," he said directly to the girl. "Thank you and good luck!"

The words meant nothing to her, only the friendliness and sincerity of the voice. No man had ever spoken to her in that tone before. And her savage heart of a child began to ache in her breast. Had he even turned and beckoned she would have followed him down the stair, into the narrow street, to the ends of the world, without a question asked. But he did not turn and

His Daughter

beckon; he went coolly and placidly down the stair.

He was the last to reach the street, at the end of which the one-horse victoria waited, since the street itself was too narrow for the passage of wheeled vehicles.

Dayton walked slowly, looking up between the tall, dark houses into a ribbon of sky spangled with stars.

The guide whispered something.

"What's that?"

"You like see that gal again sometime?"

"Certainly not," said Dayton coldly—and mechanically.

The next day, as he descended the terrace of Shepheard's Hotel, he found the guide in wait for him. In the broad daylight the creature had a peculiarly offensive and panderous cast of countenance.

"You like see that gal again?"

"I told you no. Get out!" But the man lingered.

"Well, what's the idea?" said Dayton sharply. "Didn't you hear me tell you to get out? What do you think I am?"

"Oh, kind sir," exclaimed the Egyptian, "that gal she have saved ten poun' and she have say

30

she will give him all to me if I bring you to see her."

"She will, will she?" exclaimed Dayton. And he laughed aloud and walked briskly away.

But he stopped suddenly before he had reached the end of the block and turned back. The opportunity of questioning the guide further had passed. That many-sided man was beseeching a stout American couple to let him conduct them to a bazaar where "fairly priceless" rugs were to be had for the mere asking.

It is curious that as time passed his memories of the Arab dancing girl troubled Dayton more and more instead of less and less.

The stench of the courtyard before the house, the pretentious squalor of the house itself, the beastly faces of the musicians faded; and there remained only the image of the girl herself, brown and budding, a challenge to his masculinity. If he had been brought up with a different code of morals he might very easily have yielded to the temptation of seeing her again. That she had wished to see him again was a percentage of the temptation. He was young enough to be immensely flattered, and to feel that perhaps she was really in love with him.

His Daughter

He was less tempted, perhaps, than awakened. In other words, an adolescence, subnormal because of Spartan ways of living, had passed, and Frederick Dayton was rapidly changing into a normal young man.

Cairo seemed gayer to him, more mysterious and beautiful; life larger and better worth the living. And his attitude toward life underwent rapid changes. Each morning he waked with additions to his self-confidence and with a strengthening impetus to mastery—mastery over the tools of his chosen profession, mastery over life itself.

As to his chosen profession, like many men he was weakest in that department for which he had the most natural talent. And he waked one morning with the determination to take his drawing very seriously and to make a very real accomplishment out of a mere facility.

Thereafter an ample sketch-book accompanied him on all his excursions, and he announced to the Grandisons that when he reached Paris he intended to take unto himself a studio and a master. Secretly he began to dream of being a painter in addition to being a landscape-gardener. And there was no reason why he shouldn't be a sculptor too. And, by George! since he played nicely by ear, why shouldn't he take his music seriously?

He laughed at his sudden multitudinous ambitions, but only as a matter of form. He felt within himself the strength and energy to heave a pyramid of accomplishment in the world. He would be an early Italian. Not only would he design landscapes, he would design the houses which they were to frame; the statues, the benches, and the fountains in the gardens should be from his hand, as well as the mural paintings in the house, and—yes—the door-knobs themselves and the hinges!

"Our young friend grows on me," said Mrs. Grandison to her daughter. "There's more to him than I had thought. He seemed so shy and diffident at first; but either he's changed, or else he really is shy with strangers and having gotten over that with us he's letting us see what he's really like. He talks about his future with shocking frivolity; but I believe in my heart that the world is going to hear of him one of these days, and that in his heart he knows this."

She was turning over the leaves of Dayton's sketch-book, which she had begged of him, pausing now and then over some feelingly drawn detail of architecture or some bold attempt to reproduce the life of a Cairo street.

His Daughter

"I'd like to show them to somebody who really *knows*," she said maternally.

"They're different from the things he drew in the train," said Dorothy; "those were just fooling. But these are as good as he can do. Oh, I hope he really does take a studio in Paris and begins to do real things. You must have him do a portrait of *you*, mamma."

The notion of being on intimate terms with studio life intrigued and fascinated Dorothy. At home, among girls of her own age, it would be delightful and superior to begin a Parisian anecdote with "Once in Fred Dayton's studio." It would be the choicest acquirement of her trip round the world.

Dorothy, too, was going through a period of awakening, but it was not physical as in Dayton's case. It was of the mind and spirit. She, too, began to have the impetus to mobilize her energies toward some definite end. But as no such end presented itself to her clearly, she found it difficult to make a beginning. She bought a large blank book at the stationer's and in the form of a diary attempted to reveal her own soul to herself. But certain passages which, because of their naïveté, had a real and touching value of revelation, seemed to her so silly and "ungrown-

His Daughter

upish" that she soon abandoned the attempt and destroyed the diary.

To her husband at this time Mrs. Grandison wrote:

If you are really going to join us in Paris, this letter will very likely miss you. There will be no harm done. My letter of credit holds out and we are in excellent health. We have found some old friends here and made some new ones—notably Fred Dayton, of whom I have already written to you. If Dorothy were a little older I should be worried about her. The talented youth has completely enslaved her. He can do no wrong, of course, while she, on the other hand, is frequently very humble with self-criticism. In some ways he is as young and unformed as she is, so there is nothing to worry about. I am sometimes even a little resentful that he doesn't repay Dorothy's marked attentions in kind. We shall be here ten days longer. The races begin Monday and Cairo is altogether gay and charming.

Etc., etc.

It was hard upon the sending of this letter that Dayton announced that his own days in Cairo must soon draw to an end. It had been planned that he should go on to Paris with the Grandisons and this change of determination made Dorothy secretly very unhappy.

In her own way of thinking she was genuinely

His Daughter

in love with Dayton. She had even made this confession to the defunct diary; adding that even if she ever did get over it she could never love another. That he might one day return her love did not enter her humble mind. He was much too wonderful ever to notice so commonplace an individual as herself, and now he was going away and in a few days, doubtless, would forget that she existed. . . .

She heard his laughter in the garden back of the hotel, and she put her head out of the window to find out what he was laughing at. Presently she discovered him and at the same moment he looked up and saw her.

"Come down," he called. "I've been playing hide-and-seek with the pelican."

He darted behind a tree trunk, and presently from a shrubbery the tame pelican, that lived in the garden, emerged with grotesque solemnity, hunting for him. Dorothy did not wait to see more. She hurried down-stairs and into the garden. The game, however, was over. A thin falsetto cry in Arabic had informed the pelican that his dinner of raw fish was served, and he had instantly abandoned the society of the American who had tempted him unto undignified frivolities.

"Sorry," said Dayton, "but the game's up.

His Daughter

He's gone to his dinner, and after dinner he will stand on one leg and sleep for two hours. But that's no reason why you and I shouldn't sit down on the ground and tell each other sad stories about the deaths of kings or play mumbly-peg. Which shall it be?"

He seated himself, Arab fashion, took out his pocket knife, and opened the big blade. But Dorothy neither wanted to play mumbly-peg or talk about the demises of kings. She wanted to tell Dayton how much she loved him; and of course she couldn't do that.

So she seated herself opposite him, shook her head when he offered her first turn with the knife, and looked rather wistfully into his face.

"I've been wondering," she said, "what you'll be like when we see you again."

"I shouldn't think I'd change much in a week or ten days."

"What's happened to Cairo all of a sudden that you're in such a hurry to go away? There are lots and lots of things you haven't seen."

"I'm obsessed with the idea of getting to Paris," he said, "and settling down to hard, steady work. I've loved Cairo—every minute of it. And when I've said good-by to you and your mother I 'spect I'll cry all the way to Port Said. And, speaking

37

of sad memories and bitter tears, I want a photo-
graph of *you*."

"I haven't one."

"Then we'll get up off the ground and go and
have one taken. There's a French studio down
the street. We don't need hats, do we?"

She rose at once, obedient and happy, and they
had themselves abundantly photographed with
backgrounds of camels and pyramids and without. Then, because it wasn't tea-time, they
stopped in another French place and ate charming
little cakes, and sat close to a window and watched
the life of Cairo go by.

One bit of Cairo life was an Arab girl, veiled
below the dark, smouldering eyes. She halted opposite the window, stared directly into Dayton's
face for a moment and then into Dorothy's.
Then she turned and with a savage and contemptuous shrug of her shoulders passed on.

Only the girl's eyes showed. But Dayton had
recognized her as surely as if she had appeared
as on the night when he had first seen her. And
for a few moments his heart beat with swift, hard
strokes.

"Hope she'll know us the next time she sees
us," said Dorothy. "Lordy, what manners!"

"She probably doesn't get out of the native

quarter often," said Dayton; "and white people are immense curiosities to her. I don't believe she gets much fun out of life. They don't, you know—most of them. And if she gets any fun out of staring at me I don't mind."

"I don't see why she should be so savage about it. She looked at me as if she wanted to murder me."

That second sight of the Arab dancing girl, all her beauties hidden except her eyes, disturbed Dayton even more than the first. There must have been a subtle affinity between them; for each apparently had only to look to upset the equanimity of the other. In thinking about her he made the discovery that what he imagined to be a code of morality by which all his life was to be governed existed only in his imagination. Between him and the dancing girl the obstacle was no upheaved ground of morality but rather a timidity of manners and a natural shrinking from untried experiments. In the seething crowds of the native quarter he could not hope to find her unaided. And the notion of having recourse to the guide Ali was repugnant to him. If he were to follow in the footsteps of the average man, he had the natural wish that his followings should be unknown to any one but himself and the direct object of his impulses. Nevertheless, there were times when, if the guide Ali had suddenly confronted him with "Massa want to see that gal again?" he might have flung caution to the winds and said "Yes."

Some say that propinquity has inevitable results; others hold that it is absence which makes the heart grow fonder. But the latter is only true when the effect of propinquity is maintained by the power of imagination. For the last days of his stay in Cairo the dancing girl and Dayton were seldom far apart—in Dayton's imagination.

His imagination made much of her and endowed her with allurements which she did not in reality possess. He took to wandering in the native quarter hoping for an accidental meeting. In the course of these peregrinations other adventures which presented themselves so frequently and with such ardor in that city of sudden love-affairs left him cold and even indignant. It is possible, such was his inexperience, that even the accidental meeting which, in general terms, he was actually seeking might have had the same effect on him. It is sure that she could never have seemed so desirable to him in actuality as in imagination. If he left Cairo without seeing her again he would

His Daughter

always regret it; conversely, if he did see her again he might always regret that.

After lunch on the last day of his stay in Cairo he saw Dorothy Grandison taking coffee on the terrace and joined her.

"Already," he said, "I am beginning to feel very tearful."

"Your train goes first thing in the morning?"

"Seven."

"And you go to Port Said?"

"Then across to Brindisi, then Naples, then to Rome, then to Milan, and then to Paris."

"We'll miss you dreadfully."

"I'll miss *you* dreadfully. What a lot of fun we've had! But when you get to Paris we'll begin right where we left off. You are the best little pal that ever was!"

"If only I wasn't a girl!" exclaimed Dorothy.

"Why, Dorothy," he said, "this is very sudden. Explain."

"Girls just skim the surface of things. I can't prowl around the native quarter with you and see things from the inside, or go to the Sphinx Café and hear the men who've had adventures all over the world tell about them. It's beastly to be a girl."

Dayton laughed at her; but she did not laugh.

41

His Daughter

"For instance," she said, "did you have a lot of fun the other night?"

"What other night?"

"I heard a carriage coming up the empty street. I think the noise waked me. I looked out of the window and saw you and Mr. Longstreet and some other men I didn't know."

"Why," said Dayton, "we hired a guide to show us some of the native theatres and dance-halls."

"Oh, what fun!"

"But it wasn't fun," he said seriously, "not even once. Some of it was interesting, and I suppose some of it was funny, but it was all rather sordid and tinselly, and it was long like years. And this is the proof that it couldn't have been much fun! None of us has showed the slightest inclination to go the rounds again, and the next day I was so sleepy and tired that I couldn't hold my head up."

"Are you going to the races?"

"I *can't*. I've my packing to do, and I've run up little bills here and there that I've got to run about and pay."

She looked her disappointment.

"And to-night they are giving you a farewell dinner?"

"Longstreet and some of the men I've been

friendly with. I couldn't refuse very well. But I'm not looking forward to it. I'd rather tumble into my regular place at the *table-d'hôte* next to you and your mother."

"Truly?"

"Of course. On my last night."

"Then"—her face fell—"it's good-by here and now. Mamma's gone to her room for some money to bet at the races and our carriage is waiting; and by the time your dinner-party is over I'll have been sent to bed."

She looked him full in the face, and the inner corners of her eyes filled with tears.

"But I won't say good-by now," said Dayton gravely. "I insist on seeing you again. I know how to fix it."

He gave her a sovereign.

"Bet this for me," he said; "shut your eyes and stick a hatpin into the entries for the third race. You are sure to win, and of course you wouldn't think of letting me leave without turning over my winnings to me!"

Her hand closed over the sovereign.

Then Mrs. Grandison came, and Dayton escorted the ladies to their carriage.

Sometime between their return from the races and dinner Dayton intended to take a formal

His Daughter

farewell of the Grandisons, but about six o'clock,
hot and dusty, he dropped in at the Sphinx Café
for a cocktail, found a number of acquaintances
and, as is customary on such occasions, drank
more than the one cocktail and considerably out-
stayed the time at his disposal. He returned to
the hotel, indeed, with only twenty minutes in
which to bathe and dress for dinner.

Like many young men who are not accustomed
to alcohol, Dayton had a very strong head. But
the cocktails, although they had not changed
him outwardly, had had the effect of making him
feel a little reckless and gloriously alive.

Striding along, his head high, he found himself
suddenly face to face with the guide Ali. Dayton
came to an abrupt halt; he could not have said
why.

"You like to see that gal again, kind sir?" said
Ali in a low voice.

"Yes," answered Dayton brazenly. "Why
not?"

"You come now?"

"I've got a dinner now, and then we're going to
the Sphinx. I'll tell you: you be in the garden
back of the hotel between half past eleven and
twelve. I'll come."

"Yes, kind sir."

His Daughter

" Have a carriage waiting down the street.
And look here; if you mention this to any one,
now or any time, I'll knock your head off."

" Yes, kind sir."

But no sooner had Dayton reached his room
than he began to repent of what he had done.
Shame intruded upon his mood, which had been
all made up of recklessness and desire. But at
least there was no harm done. He simply wouldn't
keep his appointment with Ali in the garden.
The laugh would be on Ali.

A dozen times while he bathed and dressed
Dayton determined to keep the appointment and
a dozen times he determined to break it. Still
undecided, he joined Longstreet in the grill.

With Longstreet were Carter, a big-game-hunt-
ing American, and Linotto, the Italian, from whom
emanated the mysterious impression that he had
something to do with international finance. Four
other men were expected, but, as these had not
yet materialized, Longstreet, as host, led the way
into the bar and ordered cocktails. These were
no sooner downed than the arrival of Evans, Tilinghast, and Carrington necessitated further hos-
pitalities.

But there was no need to wait dinner for Fitz-
roy, so Tilinghast explained. At the races Fitz-

His Daughter

roy had finally, it seemed, succeeded in getting himself introduced to the wife of the Levantine gambler. This one had promptly asked him to dinner and, considering that since his arrival in Cairo he had had eyes for nothing else, it was only natural that he had chucked Longstreet's party and accepted.

"I wouldn't mind a little *tête-à-tête* dinner with her myself," Tilinghast concluded.

"She's a screamer to look at," said Carter, "with that white streak across her black hair."

The conversation during dinner touched upon many topics—women, war, horses, the natural resources of unexploited countries, gambling, and politics. Champagne was served with the first course, and the diners became exceedingly merry and inclined to laughter.

Dayton enjoyed himself hugely. He had never in his life felt so mentally alert, so strong physically, or so entirely glad to be alive. It seemed to him that with very little effort, indeed, he was bound in a short time to become a very great artist. Outwardly calm and cool, his speech even and quiet, he was in reality enjoying a kind of seventh heaven of intoxication.

At ten o'clock the party adjourned to the Sphinx for coffee and liqueurs. Longstreet had

His Daughter

hired the up-stairs room, and there were to be dancing girls and music and more champagne. By eleven o'clock the proprietor of the Sphinx begged permission to join them. He was invited up his own back stairs with cheering and shouts of welcome.

Dayton seized the opportunity to draw Longstreet aside.

"I'm going to run over to the hotel," he said, "to finish my packing."

"But you'll come back."

"Of course."

But Dayton had no intention of coming back. Still sober in speech and appearance, the alcohol had burned his last scruples of morals and inexperience to ashes. And thoughts of the Arab dancing girl who, he had reason to believe, awaited him with the same eagerness with which he was going to her, had completely inflamed him.

But he did not at once look for Ali in the garden back of the hotel. The night was now biting cold and he went first to his rooms for a heavy overcoat and a fresh supply of cigarettes.

At the end of the corridor in which his room was located the door of the Grandisons' sitting-room was open and at the sound of his footsteps

His Daughter

Dorothy appeared in the doorway and called to him softly.

Dayton did not in the least wish to see the Grandisons at that moment, nor indeed to be seen by them. But there was no escape. And he answered Dorothy's hail with assumed cheerfulness. To his relief Mrs. Grandison was not in the sitting-room. Dorothy explained:

"Mamma said I could sit up till half past eleven to say good-by. She wanted to also, but she was dead with sleep."

"You'll say good-by to her for me, and give her my love?"

He was pleased with the sound of his own voice. It sounded natural to him and evidently it sounded natural to Dorothy, for her eyes, turned adoringly up to his, had no look of sudden questioning in them but only of constant faith. Her right hand was tightly clinched; she opened it now and offered him five golden sovereigns.

"For me?" he asked with assumed eagerness.

"For you."

"But why?"

"I picked a horse for you in the third race," she said, "according to instructions, and of course he romped in an easy winner."

Dayton at once remembered the sovereign which

His Daughter

he had given her to bet for him, and all the circumstances.

"And you picked him blindfolded with a hatpin? And you had to sit up to give me my winnings—just as I'd planned?" he laughed gleefully.

"Was the party fun?"

"Noisy and friendly, but fun. Personally I've escaped to finish my packing."

Dorothy sighed.

"It was sweet of you," said Dayton, "to sit up all this time just to say good-by to me."

"I'd have sat up all night gladly," she said, "only mamma limited me to half past eleven. And I'm afraid it's that now. And so——"

She held out her hand, and he noticed that she looked pale and tremulous.

"It's meant a lot to me," he said, "getting to be friends with you. We'll always be good friends, won't we?"

"Oh, I'm just a kid," Dorothy rebelled.

"Just a kid? Well, you'll get over that, and you know heaps more than most grown people. Good-by, Dorothy, and I wish you all the best luck in the world."

He had reached the door. She called him back. If she had been pale before she was white as death now.

"I'm not really just a kid," she said.

"I know that," he said gravely. For it was obvious to him that she was facing a crisis of some sort.

"Oh," she said, "I didn't want you to go away like that."

"No?" He came closer to her. White as she was she was bewitchingly pretty, and the strength of her feeling for him lent her face a kind of glory. Dayton was tremendously touched and moved. And he knew that he, too, was facing a crisis.

He put his arm gently around her shoulders. And she trembled at his touch.

"Do you care so much?" he said.

"And you—you don't care at all?"

"It wouldn't be right for me to say that I cared," he said; "it wouldn't be fair to you. The more I've grown fond of you, Dorothy, the more I've tried to think of you and to treat you as a little girl."

"You thought I just had a silly schoolgirl mash on you. You don't think that now?"

"No. I don't think that now. I think you really care. And as for me—well, because you are just a kid I'd promised myself that I wouldn't let myself care. But I do care. I can't help it."

But, though he did not care in the same way

that she cared, there could be no harm in letting
her think that he did—so he swiftly argued.

She had turned toward him. He folded his
other arm about her and kissed her. And she
kissed him back with all her heart and soul and
with a strength of passion that frightened him,
and the realization that he wished to keep on
kissing her frightened him still more. He shifted
his hands to her shoulders and held her at arm's
length.

"Now we belong to each other," she said
happily.

"Yes, Dorothy."

"For always and always."

He wished to say "Yes. But for heaven's
sake let's keep this to ourselves until you are
old enough to keep me from looking like a de-
signing cradle-snatcher." But he did not say
it, for something told him that he could trust
her good sense. So instead he said: "Yes, Dorothy—for always and always." And at that moment he really loved her.

"Good-by, my darling," he said, "till we meet
in Paris."

And he lifted both her hands and kissed them.
Then, because tears were rising in her eyes, he
smiled gayly.

His Daughter

"Paris isn't far off," he said, "and by the way, you haven't told me the name of the horse that won for us."

"His name was Temperament," she said, smiling through her incipient tears. "That's a funny name for a horse."

"Ali," said Dayton coldly, "is it true that dancing girl offered you ten pounds to bring me to see her?"

"Yes, indeed, kind sir."

"Well, here's ten pounds for you. I don't want you to feel that you owe me a grudge."

"And the carriage, kind sir, that is waiting down the street?"

"I guess you can afford to pay for that yourself."

Dayton turned on his heel, ascended the steps to the terrace and entered the hotel. He was in a mood of exaltation and high moral purpose.

II

DAYTON was not disappointed at learning that his sister, the Countess de Séjour, and her husband had not yet returned to Paris from their winter house near Antibes. For a few days he wanted to have Paris all to himself, and for the first three or four days, from early morning until late night, he loitered lazily and indefatigably along the streets and quays, avoiding only those parts of the city which do not belong to the French but to the whole world, and where he would have run the risk of being buttonholed by friends and acquaintances. For once in his life he wanted to be alone in Paris, to hear nothing but French spoken, to eat when and where hunger overtook him, and to dream about the great things that he was going to do.

But sometimes he dreamed about the Arab dancing girl and sometimes about Dorothy Grandison, and sometimes he dreamed about other young women who existed only in his dreams. . . .

DEAR DOROTHY:
Sudden rain has chased me under the awning of a café, and I have bought note-paper and an envelope

His Daughter

and a dark, sticky pencil. Give my love to your mother!

The rain has chased other people under the awning. To my right the broad, fat back of a neckless man; to my left the fine old Church of St. Germain des Pres; in front of me, planted on the sidewalk, a circular newspaper-stand protected by a tentlike umbrella of canvas; stand contains one red-headed girl and one very small messenger-boy. The messenger-boy is probably very witty, because every now and then he says something to the girl and she doubles up with laughter. Now I will draw a picture of them. . . .

It would be better if they hadn't found out that I was doing it, and after that I couldn't look at them often enough to make real portraits.

Except to waiters and the clerk at the hotel, I haven't spoken to a soul since I arrived. But to-morrow I hunt for a studio, and in a few days my sister comes back from Antibes and I'll have to be gregarious.

Do I have to say that I am looking forward to the arrival in Paris of Mrs. Grandison and Miss Grandison? No, I don't have to say that; but I do. The rain is letting up, and so am I.

Your faithful friend,

F. Dayton.

He addressed the letter and bought a stamp from the girl in the circular newspaper-stand. During this small transaction each displayed a certain amount of self-consciousness. The girl knew that the blond American had made a drawing of her. And he knew that she knew. The girl, however, was not self-conscious to the point of embarrassment.

"Monsieur est artiste?"

"Un peu."

He paid for his stamp, bought a newspaper in addition, wished her good day, and turned away. He had not gone far when he heard her laughing. He looked back. She and the messenger-boy were looking at him, and both were laughing. The messenger-boy looked knowing and wicked when he laughed; the girl, somewhat to Dayton's surprise, looked pretty. She had very white teeth and humorous eyes. The next morning, remembering that she had looked pretty, he walked all the way from his hotel (that of France and of England) to St. Germain des Pres and bought his morning papers of her.

He wished to know why she had laughed at him, and intended to ask her. But his courage failed him, and beyond her "Bon jour, m'sieur," and his "Bon jour, ma'm'selle," and such phrases as occur in the buying and selling of newspapers, they had no conversation.

He went away feeling rather foolish. He walked the streets, not seeking adventures, but half wishing that he was the kind of man who does seek them, and making the most of every bit of female loveliness that met his eye. But it would be unjust to give the impression that this business entirely engrossed him.

Who is there, who is not deaf, dumb, and blind, that can walk the streets of Paris with a mind concentrated upon any one thing?

That return for another look at the red-headed girl was typical of Dayton's attitude toward women at this time. That is to say, his attitude was bold—except when he was in their immediate presence. All the long walk to the news-paper-stand he had imagined conversations with the pretty vender of newspapers; but in her actual presence he had been practically tongue-tied. Is it columns you like? Well, your eyes will be distracted by the pearls in Rue de la Paix windows on your way to that column which stands in the Place Vendôme. Or, if you care for pearls, it will be the columns' turn to distract you. From morning to night not one thing interested Dayton, but a thousand things and the one. Architecture, sculpture, painting, jewel-work, furniture, hinges, knockers, bridges, gardens, iron fences and balconies, porcelain, little children, fruit-shops, the markets, the bogus antiques in the Latin Quarter, the stately proportions of public squares and buildings, those

His Daughter

thrilling perspectives to which Paris lends herself as naturally as flowers lend themselves to opening—these things complicated the feelings which the sight of a pretty face or the memory of one roused in him.

And then he found a studio which he liked—it had a view of the Luxembourg Gardens—installed himself, and, in the same spirit with which he had trained for his college teams, went to work. The De Séjours, having returned to Paris, had recommended various masters to him, and he began to draw, model, and study harmony with a perfect fury of concentration. Curiously enough the modelling, a medium which he had never before attempted, turned out to be the art for which he had the most natural facility.

He grew rapidly very jealous of his working-hours and looked upon interruptions to them with hatred. And the imminence, therefore, of Dorothy Grandison's arrival in Paris troubled him greatly. "I'll have to chuck everything," he thought, "and be at her beck and call."

It was a curious attitude; not quite so cold-blooded as it reads. He was half in love with the child. Memories of their last meeting, when she had so bravely and maturely shown her adoration for him, touched him to the quick. Some day when they were both older—well, why was he working so hard if not to be ready for the day when, she still caring and he still caring, and all their friends applauding, they should meet (she the great beauty and he the famous early Italian) before the altar of St. Bartholomew's, or some other altar just as good?

But when she and her mother actually emerged from the train which he had gone to meet, she looked so lovely and looked at him so adoringly, that he forgot all about drawing and modelling and harmony and early-Italianisms, and wanted only to give her a great hug and tell her how much he loved her, and how dreadfully he had missed her all these long, weary, lonely days!

But he did nothing of the kind. He put them in a cab, and later, when he had succeeded in rescuing their trunks from the baggage-master, followed them to their hotel—the old Chatham in the Rue Daunon—and had lunch with them, or breakfast as the French call it, to distinguish it from "little breakfast" with which meal of rolls and honey and chocolate the leisurely and intelligent French day begins.

It was not till after lunch that Dayton had a

His Daughter

word alone with Dorothy, Mrs. Grandison having excused herself on a pretext of letter-writing.

They sat in the paved courtyard of the hotel, at opposite sides of a round iron table painted green, and had a good look at each other—a good look which ended in two thoroughly charmed smiles.

"I was afraid you'd be different," said Dorothy.

She spoke in a low voice, for at one of the other tables sat a solitary old woman who had nothing better to do than to glare at them and try to overhear what they said to each other.

"You *are* different," Dayton answered.

"Older?"

"Older."

"When you care about somebody," she said, "nothing stands still. Being engaged isn't child's play, is it?"

He chuckled happily. "I was afraid maybe you'd thought over being engaged and found it wanting."

She did not trouble to shake her head; her candid and innocent eyes seemed to say: "I shall be faithful till death."

"When will you be sixteen, Dorothy?"

"Next month. And in two years I'll be of age, and you'll be famous."

His Daughter

"You're sure of that?"

"Of course."

"But you won't count on it? You'll be satisfied if I'm still working hard and trying to be, won't you?"

"Of course."

"Have you missed me?"

"Terribly. But I didn't want mamma to know about us yet, and so I tried to put on a cheerful appearance. Sometimes I couldn't go to sleep for hours. I'd stare at the dark and think of all the terrible things that might just possibly happen to you."

"Sometimes *you* keep *me* awake," he said in a reproachful voice.

"Tell!"

"I worry and worry because, looking at things from any possible slant, I can't persuade myself that I've been fair to you. You *think* grown-up and you almost look grown-up, but the fact remains that you aren't grown-up, and I've made you care for me, and it wasn't fair. But, you being you, I just couldn't help it."

"Why wasn't it fair?"

"Because your mind is growing and changing, just as the rest of you is growing and changing. And maybe what seems worth while to you now

60

won't seem worth while to you two years from
now. But because you've got the kind of character you've got you'll feel that because you've
bound yourself to me, you mustn't even try to
find out what other men are like; and I'm afraid
feeling yourself bound to me will handicap you
in all sorts of other ways. *You* don't think I've
been unfair, and maybe I make excuses for myself; but if your mother knew about us she'd be
disgusted with me, and if I was an outsider and
knew of a case like ours I'd be disgusted with
the man."

"But it isn't fair to judge one case by another.
You didn't try to make me like you. But goodness knows I tried to make you like me, and you
never even hinted you liked me until I declared
a leap-year and told you how I felt about you."

There was a short silence. Dayton had a wonderful feeling of chivalrousness and tenderness.

"How about seeing each other, Dorothy? Can
we go drives and walks together like Cairo?"

"I'm afraid not. Mamma says that in Paris
girls simply cannot go about without chaperons.
It's ridiculous, of course, but mamma is a perfectly good mamma whom to hear is to obey—
unless she interfered with something really serious.
And, besides, papa isn't coming over to join us,

His Daughter

and we'll only be here long enough to get some clothes made."

"That's bad," said Dayton simply. "I've been looking forward to weeks and weeks of just you and Paris. I'm getting to know something about Paris, and I did hope I could show you that little and that together we could go about hand in hand and find out a whole lot more. . . . I wish . . ."

"My lord wishes . . . ?"

"That you were eighteen and that your father was coming over by the next boat to look after your mother, and that they were going to give you to me to look after, and that I was rich and famous and beautiful and good."

The courtyard clock cleared its throat and rang three times.

"I have to get ready to go out with mamma," said Dorothy. "But you come up, too. We have a parlor."

To young lovers the elevators in an old-fashioned hotel are a joy forever. There is no elevator-boy. A pushed button summons the creaking, creeping cage to the floor on which you stand, you enter, you press another button and release it, then after a long interval during which the ascender seems to have been getting its forces,

His Daughter

it coughs, it trembles, and it ascends, very slowly
it ascends. The Grandisons' rooms were on the
third floor.

The Countess de Séjour had behind her two
hundred years of American ancestry. She had
therefore the American woman's gift of adapta-
bility raised to the nth power, and having married
a Frenchman she had succeeded in turning herself into a Frenchwoman.

Unlike Dayton, she was dark; her face was
charming rather than beautiful, and, although she
belonged to the ultra-fashionable hunting-set and
loved pleasure, she considered her husband's
mother, her husband, her children, and her home
of the first importance. The French have no
word for "home," but in proportion to the popu-
lation there are perhaps more real homes in
France than in any other country.

The home of the De Séjours in the Rue Barbet
de Jouy was a typical home of a fashionable and
well-to-do family.

Dayton pushed a bell in a wall and a little
iron-studded door, to the right of iron-studded
double doors tall enough and broad enough for the
passage of horses and motors, clicked and stood
ajar. He pushed it wide open and stepped over

a high sill into an ample courtyard of cobble-stones; to the right was a low building for various offices, beginning with the porter's lodge; to his left was a similar building that had been made over into an up-to-date garage. In front of this was a Rolls-Royce being gone over with chamois and a Ford touring-car being washed.

Directly across the courtyard the house door at the top of four broad steps, protected by a marquise of glass and iron, stood open, and the De Séjours' third or fourth man stood in the opening. Upon recognizing a member of the family he permitted himself to smile, not with familiarity but with friendliness and plea-sure.

"Bon jour, mon ami. Madame est chez elle?"

Madame had left word that she was to be found in the garden.

Dayton could never pass from the front door to the garden door of his sister's house without being conscious of the just and exquisite proportions of the entrance-hall, the grand staircase, and the reception-room. Stripped of their furnish-ings, and even of their lovely panellings, these spaces must still have been beautiful. A foot added here or there and the divinity of their pro-portions, their largeness and graciousness, must

His Daughter

have sunk into a very typical Fifth Avenue insignificance.

The French do not overburden their houses with accumulated purchases. And at first sight the De Séjours' reception-room might have seemed a little stiff and bare. The Louis XV chairs and sofas didn't look like comfortable machines to sit in; but they were. There were no books scattered about, no disordered ranks of signed photographs, no tables covered with armies of meaningless knickknacks requiring much dusting and mending. There weren't many things in the room, but each thing was in a place that seemed to have been especially designed for it. Twenty or thirty people, sipping cups of coffee, could move about in it at ease without having the furniture get in their way, or being nervous about unbalanced porcelains and the far-reaching lampshades of fragile lamps.

Gradually the feeling that this was not a show-room, but a room which had been much lived in, stole over one. The charming and priceless mantel-clock with the priceless and charming urns that flanked it had stood upon precisely the same spots for a hundred and fifty years. A hundred and fifty years of polite wear and tear had not made it necessary to change the tapestry which covered the chairs and sofas. It was from this room that the Revolutionary De Séjour had started on that cold and rainy journey which led to the guillotine in the great square by the river.

The garden, perhaps fifty yards square, was surrounded by tall stone walls drenched with dark English ivy. There was a simple design of broad gravel paths, flower-beds of scarlet and bright green, and the usual iron table and iron chairs which are inseparable from Paris gardens.

Bareheaded, slender, dressed very severely in black, a string of great pearls just showing where the dress was open at the throat, the Countess de Séjour, and Mouche, her fox-terrier, were alone. The countess had a plate of lump sugar on the table before her, and she was engaged in killing two birds with one stone: that is, she was teaching Mouche to speak and spoiling his digestion at the same time.

She smiled gayly at her brother and motioned him to a seat beside her.

"They are charming," she said, "and I am glad that I called. Also I have placed them. She was a Berling, one of the Hoboken Berlings, and the father used to be a great friend of Austin Mott's; they used to hunt and fish together. I am infatuated with Dorothy. And it goes without saying that you are. But I couldn't believe my ears when she told me that she was not yet sixteen. I should have guessed eighteen at the least. I hope you haven't been making love to her. I shouldn't blame you, of course, and they have plenty of money."

"It's funny about you," said Dayton. "You're not in the least sordid, and your husband takes about as much interest in money as I do in Brussels sprouts, but you are always talking money and advising me to put beauty and amiability last and to feather my nest first."

"Would you like me to ask them to luncheon? Who shall I have to meet them? Do they lean to the army or the church?"

"'Allo, Fred!" The Comte de Séjour appeared lightly descending the steps into the garden. He wore white tennis shoes, white flannel trousers, and a thick white sweater. His sunburnt face was streaming with perspiration.

"I heard you come in," he said, "but I was having a grand assault of arms with the fencing-master, and couldn't have suffered an interruption even by the President of the Republic. How are you?"

He shook hands with Dayton and straddled a

chair, facing the back, upon which he crossed his arms.

"Emily," he said, "has returned from the Hotel Chatham with most interesting reports. My dear friend, she reports that the young lady in whom you interest yourself is ravishing. The affair is serious?"

"Miss Grandison," said Emily de Séjour, "is only fifteen."

Claude de Séjour simply kissed the tips of his fingers and gazed at the empyrean. Then he turned to his wife.

"And how old were you," he said, "when I visited New York *en route* for Jackson's Hole, and never got to Jackson's Hole at all?"

"I was nearly seventeen," she said. "A whole year older. A year later we were married, and this boy just in long trousers for the first time. It was different with us,"_ said the countess. "You had something to marry on. Frederick has his way to make."

"But Miss Grandison will be rich?"

"Look here," interrupted Dayton, "let me do my own marrying, won't you?"

"First I will see this beautiful Miss Dorothy for myself."

"Seriously," said the countess, "Fred ought

not to think of marriage for years and years. He ought——"

"He ought first to sow his wild oats."

"What satanic advice!" exclaimed Dayton.

"Indeed not," said De Séjour gravely. "Sooner or later the average man sows his wild oats. And it is far kinder, far more civilized, to sow them before marriage rather than after."

"But I'm hoping," said Dayton, "that I'm not an average man. I don't believe for a minute that wild oats are either profitable or necessary."

"They are neither, perhaps," said his brother-in-law, "but in Europe we suspect the man who does not sow his of being abnormal. At least, the average man suffers sooner or later from imperious impulses, which if yielded to are of less consequence surely when they do not involve the happiness of some one else."

"I'm familiar with the continental idea," said Dayton, "but I don't believe in it."

De Séjour gave a faint shrug. "I must get into my tub," he announced, and waved them a farewell.

Dayton lingered for a few moments.

"There's a lot in what Claude says," said the countess.

"Just because he had his fling before settling

down is no reason why a man with different ideals shouldn't settle down without having any fling at all."

The countess sighed. "It is far better," she said, "that a husband should come to his bride with confessions than to the mother of his children."

"Far better," agreed Dayton, "that he shouldn't have any confessions to make to either of them."

It is true that Dayton and Dorothy Grandison were not allowed to do as they pleased—but Mrs. Grandison was a very liberal and a somewhat indolent chaperon. Her idea of sightseeing was to sit still and wait until the young people returned and told her what she really ought to have seen. In the Louvre, for instance, she would sit in front of some auburn and muscular composition of Rubens while the young people "did" the Gallery of Apollo, or she would sit in the cool of Notre Dame while they climbed one of the towers, or recline really at ease in her motor while they ransacked the book-stalls along the Quai Voltaire. And very often she retired to her room and rested from the fatigue of sightseeing while Dorothy gave Dayton tea and pleasant little cakes in the parlor.

But in the mornings, while the Grandisons were

busy with shopping and dressmaking, Dayton worked hard.

One morning, toward the end of the Grandisons' stay in Paris, he was surprised and a little troubled at receiving a note from Mrs. Grandison:

MY DEAR FRED:
May I come up? Dorothy is at the dressmaker's, and there is something that I wish very much to talk over with you.
                    In haste,
                         MARY GRANDISON.

He dashed down the one flight of stairs to the street and, somewhat embarrassed and ill at ease, helped Mrs. Grandison from her motor. But there was nothing ill at ease about Mrs. Grandison. She was in one of her most calm and cheerful moods.

"If I am breaking up work," she said, "please forgive me. I don't do it often, do I? Dorothy wants to burst in on you every morning to see what you are doing, but I won't let her."

Here, for they were nearly at the top of the stairs, her breath failed her. Dayton pushed open the door of his studio and they went in.

"I love to visit studios," said Mrs. Grandison, who had recovered her breathing powers, "but

71

that isn't why I am visiting yours. You'll not mind if I'm abrupt?"

Dayton murmured, "Of course not," and looked at her expectantly. As she did not at once go on with what she had come to say, he begged her to sit down and rest. But she shook her head, and then, smiling kindly, if a little tremulously upon the young man, she began to state her errand.

"Primarily," she said, "it's all my fault. I should have realized that Dorothy has been thrown so constantly with older people that she isn't really the child that I am always imagining she is. And I don't blame you, either. I blame myself only. But placing the blame where it belongs does not make my position any easier. I have not come here to find fault with you, my dear boy, but to ask for your co-operation and advice. What do you think we had better do?"

"I hoped," said Dayton, reddening but looking very manly and honest, "that you weren't going to find out about Dorothy and me until she was older, and I had something more tangible than ambition to offer her. On the face of it, grown men don't fall in love with girls as young as Dorothy. At first I said to myself, 'This is the kind of girl I might fall in love with if we belonged to the same generation,' and the next thing I knew

His Daughter

was—well, we did belong to the same generation, and the thing had happened to us. I know what you are thinking—that I am trying to excuse myself, and so I am in a way; but, as you say, placing the blame is of no value."

"Don't you think," said Mrs. Grandison, "that for a girl of eighteen or nineteen to care for the same man she cared for at fifteen is rather contrary to human experience?"

"Oh, yes," said Dayton, "but then Dorothy is —Dorothy."

"And yet maybe even our wonderful Dorothy isn't an exception," smiled Mrs. Grandison. "Frankly, don't you think that she ought to have the same chance that other girls of her position have?"

"I do," said Dayton, "indeed I do. And I've told her so dozens of times."

"She ought to finish growing up, to be presented to society—to have a chance—well, to find out if you are the only man in the world for her, or if there is another. And she ought to *feel* that she is free to find this out. She is very loyal. We both know that. She will keep her promise to you even if in the meantime she should find that she had been mistaken in making any such promise."

73

His Daughter

"I haven't asked for any promises, Mrs. Grandison."

"Nor made any, I dare say. But you know what I mean. And I think there should be a very definite understanding between you two that there should be no definite bond between you which, if broken by either of you, could cause the other to feel ill used."

"People can *say* that there is no bond," objected Dayton, "but if there *is* a bond? Saying that I am bound to do so-and-so isn't any different from feeling that I am bound to do so-and-so."

"It *is* different. If you say that you are bound to do so-and-so, why, so-and-so is what you will do when the time comes. But if the obligation is only one of feeling—why, then, the feeling having changed, it is no longer an obligation. Men used to feel that they were bound by the laws of the duello. They no longer feel so, and in consequence are no longer bound. I think that you and Dorothy ought to say that what is between you is not a definite, spoken engagement, but just a feeling, an inclination, which may not bring you ultimately together."

Secretly Dayton agreed with her, but he temporized.

"Have you talked with Dorothy?"

"We had it out last night," said Mrs. Grandi-

His Daughter

son, "after you had gone. But it's not a thing which a nineteenth-century parent can or ought to insist on. Still, if you can't think wisely for Dorothy now, I can't have much hope of your thinking wisely for her in the future. Her will is in your hands. . . . If this had happened to me when I was a girl my parents would have forbidden any intercourse or interchange of letters until I was old enough to know my own mind, and they would have had their way. But times have changed. Modern parents are wiser and more selfish. I should be a fool to alienate the affection that I might hope for in my old age from my daughter and my son-in-law. If my husband and I should learn that you and Dorothy had been secretly married, we would tell the world and try to make you believe that it was the very thing we most wanted. We would do that on the one chance in millions that so precocious and unconventional a marriage might turn out a success. We would not wish to be shut out from our share in that success, and we would do everything we could to help toward it."

"What a wonderful person you are!" exclaimed Dayton.

"What," she said, "do you think you will do?"

"I'd like first to talk it over with Dorothy."

"Very well; but remember that the decision is

His Daughter

with you. You are the older and the wiser. Whatever she may be a year from now, Dorothy at this moment is so crazy about you that you could make her think black was white."

"Will she know that you have been talking with me?"

"Why not? That's an honest basis to go on. Come to lunch and take her for a drive afterward. It's a lovely day. And for once I'll waive the conventions. . . . I trust you just as Dorothy does."

As he escorted her down the stairs, Dayton thought for the first time that she looked old and care-worn. He felt in those moments an immense pity for her. Though she had borne herself with great gallantry, some hint of what her real anxieties must be pierced him with remorse.

"Don't think," he said, "that I don't know how brave and kind and friendly you've been."

"Nonsense!" she said, with a twinkle in her eyes and a flash of white teeth.

"And," he faltered, "it will be a black day for me if I ever betray your trust in me."

As accurately as he could remember he told Dorothy what her mother had said.

"Is that what you think, too?" she asked.

His Daughter

"I think you should feel—well, that if some man came along and you liked him better than you do me . . ."

"*Better* than I like *you* ?"

"Dorothy, dear, I mean the way you like me, supposing that you'd stopped liking me that way. . . . I think you should feel free to like him and not as if you were committing a crime."

"But if we love each other ?" The fine, brave eyes brightened with tears.

"As long as we love each other nothing that we can say will alter the fact that we are bound to each other, so doing what your mother wishes isn't very serious and tragic, is it ?"

"Tell me again what she does wish."

"Why, I'm to say to you that if you should stop loving me, you must feel absolutely free to love somebody else."

"And I'm to say the same to you ?"

"It's just a matter of form," he said. "After all, you *are* just a kid, aren't you ? Your mother wants you to have the same chances that you would have had if you and I had never met. She wants you to come out, by and by, and have your fling, and dance all night, and make friends, and be loved by all the gentlemen, and I think . . . I think she's right."

His Daughter

"But where will you be when I come out, and until I do?"

"The idea is for me to keep out of the way, I suppose," he said dismally. "But surely after a year or so, if you still feel the way you do now, your mother—they—would be willing to have me come around. . . . It's a sort of probation. We're not disapproved of or threatened or anything like that. We're simply asked to acknowledge what is the truth: that you are unusually young. And we are asked to look at our case from an outsider's point of view and decide on the sensible thing to do."

Their taxi turned slowly into one of those narrow and winding roads through natural woods which are so characteristic of the Bois de Boulogne. The trees were all ashimmer with the vivacious greens of early spring and there was a merry twittering of birds.

"I suppose," said Dorothy, a little sullenly, as if she had been argued into something against her will, "that from an outsider's point of view mamma is right."

Dayton nodded sagely. "And she leaves everything to us," he said.

"And I," said Dorothy, "leave everything to you."

His Daughter

After a considerable silence, Dayton put his arm around her, and instantly she leaned against him. Then very tenderly he said:

"I love you with my whole heart and soul."

"And I," she said, "love you with my whole heart and soul."

Then he kissed her. And then he said, his voice husky:

"But we are *not* engaged, my own dear. Oh, no, indeed we are not. You have made me no promise . . . no promise at all. And you are going back home and I'm going to stay on here for about a year, so's not to be always popping up when I'm not wanted. And we are going to write to each other; but not every day, only once in a while like friends, not like lovers, just to say how we are and what we are doing. And you mustn't try to stop loving me any more than you must try to keep on loving me. You must just try to keep on going as if I'd never happened, and then, bimeby—some day—all will be well with us again."

She leaned closer to him, and his arm tightened about her. And then she turned up her face to his, tears in the eyes and a smile on the mouth, and said:

"Don't let's stop being **engaged until we are** out of this wood."

His Daughter

And there was something at once so touching and gallant in her voice that tears came into Dayton's eyes, and almost he wished then and there to die while heroically defending her from some evil or other. Mingled with his love for her was an even tenderer and more exalted feeling. He felt a little as if she were his daughter.

Paris was empty. It was as empty as are those little silk or satin jewel-boxes which abound in the upper drawers of bureaus, and from which the jewel has been taken.

Dorothy Grandison had gone home to America.

Dorothy Grandison had gone home to America, and Paris was empty.

It remained empty for about a week. Dayton kept telling himself how much he loved Dorothy and how necessary to his happiness was her daily nearness; but what he told himself along these lines was not the whole truth. In spite of his very natural wish to be the faithfulest and loneliest lover in the world's history, the empty city of Paris began to fill up with color and beauty and charm, with voices and faces.

His was not the kind of heart which, fed upon absence, grows fonder and fonder. He lived a crowded life in which, by slow stages, the photo-

His Daughter

graphs of Dorothy which he had upon his dressing-table came to play a greater part than his memories of her. And at last, not without self-contempt, he came to realize this. He had not tired of her, and if she had been present he must still have been in love with her. What was wrong, then? Only this—that he had never loved her in the same way that she loved him. She had driven nothing out of him and refilled the vacuum with herself.

But where an individual had failed the sex of that individual had succeeded. Though a particular romance had not enmeshed Dayton eternally, romance herself had him thoroughly in her net. He was, in short, tremendously sentimental.

May passed and June. The thermometer climbed steadily. There were breathless days reeking of hot asphalt. The outlines of buildings and monuments were softened by a kind of dancing, gyrating aura. The children who played in the Luxembourg Gardens looked pale and hollow-cheeked. The morning sun beat upon the flat roof of Dayton's studio and turned his working-hours into a kind of unprogressive nightmare.

The tools of the various crafts which he was attempting to master slipped in his fingers. Wherever his hand rested there remained a spot dark with moisture. It was like trying to work in the

His Daughter

hot room of a Turkish bath. No wonder he had rented that studio cheaply.

His progress until now, especially in modelling, had been steady and stimulating. But he had come to that pass—a pass to which all artists are subjected now and then—when his hands seemed to be all thumbs and his brain no more capable of concentration than a dish of hot oatmeal.

Everything went wrong. Models, lured by the thought of a cool day in the country, either sent word that their grandmothers were suddenly dead or simply did not keep their appointments at all. His drawing-master departed suddenly for the Brittany coast, and the organist who was teaching him the elements of harmony left as suddenly for a good cooling off in the Austrian Tyrol.

For their children's sakes the De Séjours had left Paris at the first blast of the July heat, and Dayton was strongly tempted to follow them into the country. Only his innate stubbornness prevented. He had announced more than once that he would stick to his last all summer, weather or no weather, and he felt that any backing down would be an abject confession of weak-mindedness.

One afternoon about three o'clock the unwinking, staring heavens became suddenly overcast,

His Daughter

and the faint, far-off mutterings of thunder were heard. The storm did not come up quickly, but slowly and with dignity, and with great thoroughness. The streets of Paris and the parks became suddenly alive with people hurrying for shelter, and since his working light was gone Dayton seated himself by an open window to see the storm break upon a populace that, confident in the promise of a glaring noon, had sallied forth without umbrellas or rain-coats.

After an interval of livid purple darkness great drops of water began to fall; so big were these drops that it seemed to Dayton as if each one would have half-filled a coffee-cup. He put out his hand and one, icy cold, splashed upon it. He laughed aloud; the tension under which he had been living was instantly relieved.

Whirling dust and bits of paper rose in a column and rushed along the sidewalks. The wind roared and whistled, and then, literally with a crash, rain fell and instantly the whole street was awash, and the people who remained for a few seconds before getting shelter under the deep archways of doors and gates were wet to the skin.

A man, a stout woman, a young woman, and two small boys crowded into the narrow archway that was directly below Dayton's window. There was a simple smartness about the top of the young woman's hat that attracted him. He wondered what her face was like.

For an hour the man, the stout woman, the young woman, and the two small boys were held prisoners by the wall of rain. Then, as this grew thinner, one of the small boys emerged as suddenly from the archway as if he had been shot out of a gun, and, shielding his head with his left forearm, and further seeking to save himself from a wetting by dodging and twisting, ran furiously round the nearest corner and disappeared. Soon after the other small boy departed. His method was all his own; he made himself as small as possible and moved very cautiously, as if he were afraid of waking the baby. Perhaps he thought that if the rain didn't see him or hear him it wouldn't wet him.

The sky by now was very much brighter, and the rain no heavier than an April shower. But what there was of it, in spite of occasional flashes of sunlight, persisted. The stout woman and the man left at the same time, but in opposite directions. And there remained in the shelter of the archway only the young woman.

The storm being no longer interesting, various speculations concerning her began to occupy

His Daughter

Dayton's mind, and, having nothing to go on but the top of her hat, he concluded that she was attractive. He wished that she would come out from under the archway so that he could have another look at her. But although the rain was now no more than a sprinkle she remained under shelter.

"She must hate water like a hen," thought Dayton; "or maybe it's her best hat."

He leaned far out of the window, but could see only the toe of her right shoe. Her fear of being even lightly sprinkled touched his sense of humor, and it was not until the storm which had swept over Paris began to return and the rain to fall more briskly that he began to feel sorry for her.

Acting upon a sudden thought, he took his umbrella, ran lightly down the stairs to the entrance-hall, and opened the front door. She turned toward him and he recognized the red-haired girl who sold newspapers near the Church of St. Germain des Pres. The recognition was mutual. It was almost as if they were old friends. "Oh!" they said, "it's you."

Then a lameness, to which it was frequently a victim, a kind of general rheumatism, suddenly crippled Dayton's French. And he said "I— you—the rain—for you—the umbrella——"

"How kind you are!" said the girl. But she looked doubtfully at the umbrella and still more doubtfully at the weather.

"I was to meet some friends," she said; "we were going down the river for dinner, and—well, you see I wanted to look nice, and a dressmaker who is a friend of mine loaned me this pretty dress. If it got spoiled I'd have to pay for it, and I *can't*."

Having told him her troubles frankly, she smiled them away. She was very pretty when she smiled.

"If I got you a cab——"

But she shook her head firmly. Evidently the price of that was also beyond her; and somehow Dayton did not like to offer to pay the fare for her.

"It can't rain forever," she said.

Dayton had recovered from his lingual rheumatics.

"I'm not sure," he said; "it's falling harder all the time. At least come into the hall and sit down. Or better, if *you* don't mind, come up to my studio and I'll give you a cup of tea, or chocolate, if you'd rather."

"Shall I?" she said, smiled, hesitated, looked him suddenly in the face, and said gravely: "Thank you. How kind you are!"

His Daughter

"It isn't much of a studio," he explained; "it's rather bare, but there's one really comfortable chair and you've been standing so long you'll like that."

He threw open the door of his studio and repeated: "It isn't much of a studio."

Then—for her presence really embarrassed him—he began to make a great to-do with preparations for tea.

"I'm glad you chose my door for a shelter instead of somebody else's," he said.

"So am I," said she. "This chair is very comfortable."

"So *that's* why you are glad!" He lighted the lamp under the teakettle and turned his smiling face toward her.

"You and I," he said, "are old friends. Don't you think we ought to know each other's names? Mine's Dayton—Frederick Dayton."

"Mine," she said, "is Claire—Claire D'Avril."

"That's a *lovely* name!" exclaimed Dayton. "Claire D'Avril!"

"It's a little theatrical, don't you think?"

But he shook his head. "No," he said, "it isn't. It's what you just naturally would be called." And his attention became riveted on the tea-caddy, the lid of which had jammed.

His Daughter

"It's raining as hard as ever," she said.

"Good!" said Dayton. "It prolongs this extremely pleasant visit. Are your feet wet?" She shook her head.

"Sure?"

"A little splashed, but not wet."

Her presence no longer embarrassed him. It began to seem quite natural that she should be sitting in his big chair, chin on hand, watching him make tea. Her presence had become extremely agreeable to him. There was something very wholesome and direct about her. And when she smiled she was really pretty.

"The other day," he said suddenly, "you laughed at me—you and your friend, the small boy. Why was that?"

She laughed at him again. "It was only to make you look round. He said: 'Laugh and he'll look round.' And we laughed and you did, and that made us laugh still more."

"Why did you want me to turn round?"

"My small friend said you were cross-eyed, and I said you weren't. And you aren't."

Rested and stimulated by two cups of indifferent but strong tea, Claire D'Avril, under Dayton's guidance, which consisted very largely of explana-

His Daughter

tion and apologies, made a tour of inspection. She made him show her all his drawings and all his modellings. She even gave a grave and sweet attention to a choral which he had written (holding it upside down the while), and she touched the keys of the piano very timidly, and her face, at the ensuing discord, took on an expression that was akin to ecstasy.

Presently, for it was growing dark, Dayton lighted candles and pulled the shades over the windows. It was still raining hard, and he wondered what Claire D'Avril was going to do about it.

"I love to have her," he thought; "she's the first really lovely thing that's happened to me for weeks and weeks; but I ought not to let her stay."

She stood in front of his big easel, her head on one side, her hands lightly clasped behind her back, and for the first time it occurred to him that he would like to draw her. He liked her poise, her unaffected gracefulness, the high but not stiff carriage of her head.

"Some day," he said, "if I ever get so that I'm any good, I'd like to do a portrait of you. Have you ever posed?"

She shook her head.

"I have a friend who is a model," she said,

His Daughter

"but hers is a sad history of one cold in the head after another. Yet she has a pretty figure and is well paid, so she can't afford to give up posing."

"I didn't mean the kind of posing that leads to a cold in the head," Dayton laughed, and stammered into an abrupt change of subject.

"Where do you live?"

"With my uncle in the Rue Centrale," she said. "My father and mother are dead. But I earn my board by selling newspapers and magazines."

"Won't your uncle be worried about you?"

"Oh, no; he thinks I am down the river with my friends. And if we had gone I shouldn't have returned till late—very late. He never worries. If I never came back at all he would simply say it was what he had always predicted. Every day when I go to work he says: 'Well, good-by and good luck if I should never see you again.' But that is very natural. Among the poor—*que voulez-vous !*" She shrugged her shoulders.

"He leaves you absolutely free to lead your own life?"

"Of course. I'm free as air. It is very nice. It is also very lonely sometimes."

"You ought to marry and have a home of your own."

"I could have married," she said. "It was

understood; but while we were engaged we got to like each other less and less instead of more and more, so it's just as well nothing came of it. But it would be pleasant. I don't like selling newspapers. The hours are so long and you stand up so much. I like to cook and sew and go to market. And I am an enemy of dust."

"Speaking of cooking," said Dayton, "it's getting on toward dinner-time. Tea wasn't very solid. What do you say? There's a nice little restaurant only a few blocks away—Gibier's."

"But the rain?"

"You'll stay here while I go for a taxi. After dinner I will drive you home. And if your pretty dress gets even one splash of water on it, why I'll be responsible to the dressmaker."

"You are very rich for an artist."

"I have more money than many artists," he said, "for the simple reason that I am not an artist."

So presently he put on his rain-coat and took his umbrella and sallied forth in search of a taxi, while Claire D'Avril settled herself luxuriously in the big chair and thought long thoughts.

"He treats me as if I were a vicomtesse," she said. "It is very pleasant with him. This room could be made very charming and clean. He is

His Daughter

very timid. He is not like other men. He has not tried to take advantage of me. I shall ride in a taxicab, and dine at Gibier's. I am glad I am nicely dressed. He will not be ashamed. I don't think he will ever be a great artist. He has a little talent, but not much. Anybody could see that he has put one of that old man's ears too high. . . . I wonder what he would say if I asked him to let me stay? I should like to live with him, because he is so gentle. Was it altogether accidental that I took refuge under his doorway instead of another; or was there some unfathomable design about it? It is easy to see that he wastes his money. I'd be a real bargain for him if he only knew it. . . ."

At this moment Dayton returned. He looked at her with pleasure. She looked very much at home in the big chair.

"Some people," he said, "like paintings and tapestry and gilt furniture, but to my mind nothing makes a room look as dressed up as the persons in it, if one is a pretty girl."

He placed his hat on his heart and made her a gallant bow.

"The taxi of madame is at the door," he said.

She rose, but with evident reluctance.

"It is nice here," she said. "I have been happy."

His Daughter

"It's been nice having you," he said.

At the door she turned lingeringly as if to take in all the details of the place and impress them on her memory.

"How many rooms are there?" she asked.

"Just a bedroom and a bathroom besides the studio and a sort of glorified clothes-closet."

"And there is a fireplace so that you will be warm in winter. It is very nice."

Claire D'Avril sighed, but as they walked slowly down the stairs she held her head very high.

"You are different from other men," she announced.

"In what way?"

"You are generous. Other men are selfish."

"All other men?"

"Yes," she said, "all the others."

For the brief passage of the sidewalk he made her put on his rain-coat and at just the right angle he held the umbrella to shield her hat from the rain. Not a drop fell on her borrowed plumage.

"It will be fine in the restaurant," she announced. "Perhaps some of my customers will be there. They will say: 'Look at Claire D'Avril in a blue-silk dress eating dinner with the American nobleman!' I am glad it rained, and that I did not go down the river with my friends. I am happy."

His Daughter

Dayton was less happy. Gibier's was his favorite "hang-out." There, nearly always alone, and never in the company of a prepossessing young female, he took all his meals. The present adventure, innocent as it was, would give rise to comments and asides among the other *habitués* of the place. And when he made his "grand entrance," Claire D'Avril at his side, he would blush and feel foolish. He knew he would.

And he did. But the waiter and *habitués* took no more notice of Dayton (apparently) than if he had been alone. Only madame (the real proprietor, her big husband to the contrary notwithstanding), fat to bursting, seated at her high desk in the corner, greeted them with her warmest and most approving smile. And she said to herself: "I am so glad. He has always seemed so lonely."

Dayton's embarrassment was short-lived. He began to enjoy himself. Until he contrasted her with some of the other women diners, he had not realized how very smart and presentable Claire D'Avril was. The rosy lighting of the room was very becoming to her. She had a lovely skin. He was proud of her. He would ask her to dine with him again sometime. Gayety and happiness gave her face a kind of childlike radiance. And her delight and pride were almost without bounds when he told her that the sparkling stuff in her glass was champagne.

An orchestra of three pieces played softly. Claire D'Avril had shaken off all the dust and weariness of this world. She was in heaven. Dayton was a god. Fifteen cents here—twenty cents there—a small fortune for a bottle of champagne! It was nothing to him! If not a god, he was at least some great, mighty lord. Also he was very beautiful. Blessed is the lot even of the dog of such a man. . . .

The coffee-cups were empty. Dayton's cigar was only an inch and a half long. Many of the tables were empty. It was half past ten. The big clock on the wall said so. Claire D'Avril sighed.

"I suppose," she said, "it's time to wake up."

"You have the nicest way of putting things," he said.

"But it *has* been like a dream!" she said. "I have been very happy."

"We'll do it again, then," said Dayton. "Yes—yes—please!"

The rain was over. Stars were shining. Claire D'Avril bit her lips. She had so looked forward to one more taxi ride. Now she would have to walk. But not so. Well and truly did the great

95

mighty lord hail a passing taxi and chivalrously and courteously did he put her into it, and, following, sat down beside her.

To the house of Claire's uncle in the Rue Centrale was a long distance. For a time you followed the river, then you passed through a labyrinth of narrow, twisting, fifteenth-century streets, and then, unless you knew your Paris by heart, you found yourself in a quarter of the city that was new to you, a quarter dull, rectangular, poor, and uninteresting. But it had its advantages. Rents were very low.

Either the young people were talked out, or had come to that pleasant pass in human relations when comparative silence is the most agreeable eloquence.

Claire D'Avril leaned back luxuriously, her eyes half-closed, her lips parted in a ghost of a smile. Whenever the taxi passed through the illuminated area about a street lamp Dayton stole a look at her. She had a face of which you would not soon grow tired. Her dominant expression was candor and tolerant good humor. Now and then they exchanged remarks.

"It is very far to bring you. I am sorry."

"But I'm enjoying myself."

His Daughter

"It will be very expensive. I could have walked."

The taxi stopped. The driver leaned from his seat and spoke through the open window:

"Do you know the way?"

"Use the left . . . the next turn. Then straight on. I will tell you when to stop."

She sighed. "We are nearly there."

"Are you sorry?"

"Yes."

For some time Claire D'Avril had been making it obvious to Dayton that she enjoyed being with him; that the day had been a day to mark with a white stone; and that the return to the house of her uncle had its tragic side.

"When I get back to the studio, it will seem very empty," he said.

"You must tell the wife of the *concierge* to dust in the corners," said she. "I gave one look and I said to myself: 'Either the wife of the *concierge* is an invalid, or else she is not a good woman.' Also, because you are rich, you should always have a few flowers. Then it will not seem so empty."

Dayton bowed gravely. "I hear, and I obey," he said.

Claire D'Avril leaned from the window. "Stop!" she said. "We're there."

His Daughter

Dayton helped her out. "Good night," he said. "Thank you for a charming evening. Good luck! *Au revoir!*"

The driver faced around so that he could better view a scene which caused him infinite astonishment and amusement. His eyes became round as two inflamed saucers and he stuck his tongue into his cheek. His fares were actually saying good-by to each other. That was about the last thing he had expected.

"Thank you for everything," said Claire D'Avril, "and *au revoir!*"

She turned abruptly and disappeared into a dark archway.

"Not pretty enough?" asked the driver.

Dayton did not answer this impertinent question. He merely gave the address of his studio.

Claire D'Avril rang a bell. The door confronting her gave out, after a long interval, a sudden alarming click, and stood ajar. She closed it carefully behind her, and meditatively climbed four flights of steep, narrow stairs.

Her mother's brother, Jules Legros, a lean, nervous little man, was in his workshop, a room no bigger than an average bathroom. By the light of a single gas-jet he was delicately removing a very small rust stain from a splendid sword-hilt

His Daughter

of carved steel. His business in life was a business which is almost extinct. He was an armorer. He had entire charge of Baron de Rible's astounding collection of weapons and coats of mail, and except for its chief treasure, a sword-hilt by Cellini, there was no piece in that collection which, given time, he could not have duplicated. He had no peer in all Europe. And upon an income of something over a dollar a day he supported an incompetent wife and three young children.

"Good evening," he said, with cheerful cynicism. "I did not expect you in so early. I thought perhaps you would not come back at all."

"We did not go down the river because of the rain . . . my aunt and the children?"

He tossed his head toward the door at the farther end of the workroom and remarked that the sardines were safe in their box.

"You'll ruin your eyes."

"This is a special job. I am to be paid a little extra. The baron has just bought this sword. It is of the most splendid. He wishes to exhibit it to a friend. The extra money will come in very handy, because madame your aunt announced to me only this morning that there is to be another sardine."

"But that's a tragedy."

99

His Daughter

Jules Legros shrugged his shoulders and held the hilt of the sword very close to his eyes.

"The poor little things!" he said. "They have a right to be born."

"But four children! It's unheard of! I think you and my aunt ought to be thoroughly ashamed of yourselves!"

"And you," said Legros, imperturbably changing the subject, "since you did not go down the river? You dined somewhere, I suppose?"

"With an American gentleman," she said.

"They are very rich, these Americans," commented her uncle. "It is a very rich country, and very immense. It is twice as big as France. I could make my fortune selling imitation weapons to Americans. They are at once open-handed and gullible."

She leaned against the work-bench and vivaciously and with much detail recounted her adventures.

"It is these sudden, unlooked-for pleasures that give spice to life," said her uncle. "You now not only have something out of the ordinary to look back upon, but the possibility of future extraordinary happenings to look forward to. You have ridden in a taxi, not once but twice. You have drunk champagne. It's immense. And now it is late. Go to bed."

His Daughter

"Uncle," she said, "what will become of me when the new sardine arrives? There isn't room *now*."

"It is a pity that your marriage fell through."

"I am terribly in the way. I know that. You must hate me."

"On the contrary, my child, I love you very well. You are a good girl. Sometimes I think, considering your station in life, that you are too good for your own good." And he cackled mildly at his pleasantry.

"And now go to bed—while there is still room."

Claire D'Avril was at her news-stand bright and early. She hoped against hope that Dayton would come to her stand to buy a paper. She was in a merry humor. Certain men who bought papers of her solely for the opportunity thus afforded of making love to her, were treated to some very rough-and-ready examples of her wit and self-reliance. Her vocabulary and her breadth of mind and knowledge would have horrified Dayton.

She was no longer his gentle companion in blue silk, but a very plainly dressed young woman, who, if she had not been brought up in the gutter, had always lived where she could see and hear what was going on in that metaphoric place.

His Daughter

Just when she had given up all hope of seeing Dayton that morning he appeared, not strolling, as was his habit, but walking with long, energetic strides. Her heart gave a sudden strong leap.

"Good morning, Mademoiselle D'Avril," he said. "I have come for my paper. *Le Matin,* please."

Without taking her happy, smiling eyes off Dayton, Claire D'Avril separated a copy of *Le Matin* from a diminished pile and handed it to him.

"Your uncle wasn't angry?"

"Oh, no! I told him all about everything, and he was pleased that I had been happy."

"What do you do when you want to take a day off? Is there some one who looks after the news-stand for you?"

Claire D'Avril's smile grew more bright. For Dayton's questions seemed to indicate some sort of a delectable invitation.

"To-morrow," he said, "I am going to Fontainebleau for the day. Would you care to come?"

Dayton had not intended to ask her to go with him. The wish to do so had come to him suddenly, while he stood looking at her.

"Monsieur," she said, "I should have to come

His Daughter

just as I am. I have no better dress than this, and I have already returned the blue dress to my friend. You would be ashamed to be seen with me. And so"—her lower lip quivered—"I mustn't think of going."

"What nonsense!"

But she was very firm. The more she thought of it, the less she could tolerate the idea of disgracing him in the eyes of the world. What he felt to be sheer stubbornness and false pride nettled Dayton.

"It's for the pleasure of your company that I'm asking you," he said, "and for no other reason. But you don't care to come. Well, I'm sorry."

"*Please* don't be angry with me," said Claire D'Avril. "It's—you haven't quite understood. It's—" She spoke very rapidly and in a low voice. "When people see a man and a girl going about together, they—well, if the man is well dressed and the girl is shabby—they, the people, that is, think of that man with contempt. They say: 'He is mean to her.' Now, last night at the restaurant, when the people saw me in that fine blue-silk dress, they said: 'There is a man who is good to his little friend. And I who know how kind you are and how generous, cannot bear to have anybody think differently about you. There! That is why I will not go to Fontainebleau with you in these shabby clothes! Now do you understand?"

"Why, yes," said Dayton, "I think I do. But what total strangers think about me doesn't interest me very much. Still, if it interests you—" He hesitated. He was afraid that if he bluntly offered to buy her a pretty dress she would be insulted. "If," he said, "you had a pretty dress, you wouldn't be ashamed to be seen with me? But you can't afford to buy such a dress. . . . Now, look here. My French is execrable. You shall give me lessons in conversation. I will pay so much for the lessons, and I will advance my teacher enough money to buy her a charming costume. Now, please don't say 'No.'"

But Claire D'Avril did not say "No." A look of ecstasy came into her eyes. She felt as if she had peeped into heaven.

"Yes! Yes!" she exclaimed. "I will give you lessons. It is wonderful!"

The next day they went to Fontainebleau. Claire D'Avril had bought the blue-silk dress and the smart little hat that went with it. They visited the palace, they had a delicious lunch, with a small bottle of red wine, under a grape-arbor, and afterward they strolled in the cool forest. She amused Dayton immensely, interested him, and charmed him. She was immensely companionable.

They returned to Paris and had dinner at the Tour d'Argent. And afterward he drove her home.

"It's been a very short day, Claire," he said. "I hate to say good-by."

"I, too," she said.

And after that, for several blocks, there was a kind of charged silence. He was growing fond of her. And he knew it. He was beginning to have a feeling of responsibility toward her; a wish to make her life easier, to spend a little money on her. The cab stopped.

"When am I to have another lesson, Claire?"

"When you wish."

He hesitated for a moment, and then said:

"To-morrow?"

"At what time and where?"

"If I come to your news-stand for you, the café will begin to talk, and that might not be agreeable for you. Could you come to the studio about four o'clock? I think it would be fun to drive in the Bois and dine at the Cascades."

"At four, I shall come."

His Daughter

"Good.   And good night."

"Good night."

Youth is swift.   And it got so that either Dayton himself, or his thoughts, were with Claire D'Avril almost all the time.   She was no longer merely a pretty girl and an amusing companion. There were moments when she seemed really beautiful in his eyes, and he had impulses almost violent to take her in his arms and kiss her.

Dorothy Grandison's grave eyes, of which many pairs looked at him from his bureau, no longer troubled him.   He was as free from any influence she had ever had over him as if they had never met.   Dorothy had been an episode.   She was only a child.   Probably she, too, was forgetting him.   How wise Mrs. Grandison had been about the whole thing!   He was very grateful to her. . . . That Arab girl in Cairo had left a more vivid impression upon his mind than Dorothy had succeeded in making. . . .   But Claire D'Avril! . . .   Other artists . . .   Why, it was the custom of the country. . . .   People neither thought well nor ill of such relationships.   They simply did not think about them at all . . . to have her always with him . . . not to be always waiting and waiting, and almost at once to be saying good-by. . . .

His Daughter

But he could not bring himself to say the words which might have altered their relationship. They stuck in his throat. He would start the day firmly resolved to get the matter settled one way or the other. But when the moment for speaking out seemed to have arrived, his courage failed him.

With his work he was now making no progress. His heart had abandoned all co-operation. It was, so to speak, always running off to be with Claire —while he remained numb and heartless to confront the challenge of the drawing-paper or the wet clay. But if Claire came to live with him all would be well. She would be an inspiration; his work would be a miracle of progress.

He was glad to think that he had never fallen into any chance intrigue. Had Claire? he wondered. Very likely. He did not wish to know. He would never ask her. He would always be good to her, always tender. And if they ever did have to part, he would manage to take care of her. But he could not think about parting. He loved her so dearly that such thoughts stabbed like knives. . . . There would be no parting. Time would stand still. It would be always summer.

Claire D'Avril had made an unconscious but

thorough study of such phases of living and manners as had come under her observation. The women whom she admired, whether married or not, were good housewives, who made their men comfortable and saved their money for them; to belong to the man she loved, and to sacrifice herself in every way for his welfare and comfort, was, roughly speaking, her idea of the whole duty of woman. She was very ardent, very sentimental, and very practical. From any sum of money she could extract the last least portion of its purchasing power. And she knew her potential value either in real marriage or in one of those relationships so usual on the Continent, and which perhaps may best be described as trial marriages. She knew of one trial marriage which at the end of eighteen years had been changed into a real marriage.

If she should become Dayton's mistress, she would not lose caste. Her uncle, a good and upright man, might tease her, but in his heart he would feel that she had done well for herself.

Already her influence over Dayton had transformed the studio. He had bought two or three good pieces of furniture and a really ancient and splendid rectangle of yellow brocade. He had learned that there is such a thing as dust, and the

most likely places to look for it.   He had bought
a number of flowering plants in pots, so that the
great room, formerly so bare and gray, had bright
color now and was very livable.

Claire came often to the studio.   He was doing
a head of her which, if not a delightful picture,
gave promise of being a good likeness.   She preferred the studio to the Bois, to the Luxembourg
Gardens, to Gibier's, to the Tour d'Argent, to the
Forest of Fontainebleau or any of their other
haunts. It gave her proprietary feelings.   She
no longer introduced changes with: "Don't you
think *you* had better do so and so?" but with:
"Don't you think *we*," etc.   He was continually
asking her advice, for the sheer pleasure of having
her give it.   And he always took it, sometimes
for the sheer pleasure of giving her pleasure.   If
his drawing was standing still, his French at least
was going forward by leaps and bounds.   It would
never be French French, but already there was
plenty of it, and each day there was more.

The fifteenth of August was one of the most
important days in their lives. The morning was
hazy and sultry. Dayton got it over with as
best he could, and the early hours of the afternoon. She was not coming until six.   They were

His Daughter

going to dine somewhere on the other bank of the river, and later to see a very famous actor in "Le Monde on l'on s'Ennuie."

He had told her to come in a taxi. Now and then he looked out of the window; and all the time, in his subconsciousness, he was listening for the burr of the motor. But Claire, economical to the core, except on the occasions when Dayton himself could share in the extravagance, had walked.

There was a light knocking and the door of the studio very slowly opened.

She was wearing the famous blue-silk dress (it was wonderful how perennially fresh she kept it), and her face, all alight with the pleasure of the moment, was ravishingly pretty.

"Here I am!" she said.

"And you walked, you little niggard!" He smiled upon her with much tolerance. "Shall we start?"

"Let me sit down for five seconds. I ran up the stairs. I'm all out of breath."

So she sat down for "five seconds" and allowed her eyes to roam triumphantly among the various improvements which she had effected.

"How did you leave the family?"

"Ah, the poor things! When it is hot like this,

they are so crowded. Tinon has a frightful fever blister. He cannot leave it alone and it gets worse and worse. It is cool here."

"Cool," said Dayton, "and at the moment pleasant. But during the day it has been empty and lonely and disagreeable. I have worked hard and I accomplished nothing."

"You are a perfect child," she said. "When you are alone you don't know what to do. . . . Well, don't stand there looking at me like that! I'm rested. Shall we start?"

"I'll go after a cab."

"Let's go together. It's not far to the cab-stand. And you look so magnificent in those clothes that I don't want to miss a single moment of reflected glory."

All through dinner, and all through the play, Dayton was curiously reserved and silent. Usually he entered into the spirit of things with all his heart. She wondered what ailed him and proposed at the first opportunity to find out.

As a matter of fact, Dayton had made a firm resolution, and it was this which weighed upon his spirits. He was ill-at-ease and very nervous. For he had come to a definite conclusion that either his relations with Claire must change or cease. He couldn't work and he couldn't sleep; but if she wouldn't have him, if he went away, making a great effort to put behind him all memories of her, he might win back to cool sanity.

In short, he had determined to speak.

The play over, they walked slowly along the sidewalk looking for a cab. Having found one, Dayton gave the driver, not the address of Claire's uncle, but of the studio. As he did so his voice shook a little and his heart leaped in his breast. He stole a look at Claire D'Avril. She did not seem to have heard.

When the cab stopped opposite the doorway in which she had taken ˄refuge from the rain, she made no comment. Dayton opened the door with his latch-key and silently and very slowly they climbed the one flight of stairs to the studio.

Having entered, Claire spoke for the first time. Her voice shook a little.

"It's nice here," she said.

Dayton left her alone for a moment, without explanation. He stalked into his bedroom, gathered together with a kind of passion all his photographs of Dorothy Grandison and shoved them into the back corner of a drawer under a pile of neckties. Then he went back to Claire.

She had not moved. He went up to her quickly

and caught both her hands in his. He meant to
speak gently. But he had to force his voice, and
the result was to make it sound rough and imperious.

"If you want me to get a cab and send you
back to your uncle's, say so quickly," he said.

"But I don't," she said, in a small voice. "I'd
rather stay with you."

III

CLAIRE D'AVRIL had gone; but the studio was not empty. She had gone, not as the parting guest goes, but as one who sallies forth briefly from a refuge—from a stronghold, and who will soon return. She would not return because she was invited to, but because she had a right to; the studio was hers now, to do with as she pleased. And she intended to make a home of it.

So, very proudly and with a new and wonderful look in her eyes, without compunction or regret, without fear, confident of the future, confident in the goodness of the human heart, having been tenderly embraced at parting, she sallied forth into the lovely sunshine, and, having hailed a taxicab, was driven in state to the home of her uncle.

She was not early enough in the day to catch her aunt and the children. She was not sorry.

Jules Legros, bent over his bench, straightened his thin back with an effort and looked at her curiously. She had expected a cynical greeting. She was surprised at detecting in his voice a note, not altogether new, but very rare, of sorrow and pity.

"You have come for your things, I suppose, my poor little Claire?" he said.

"Yes, uncle, and to tell you of my great happiness."

"Happiness is like sunshine on an April day. Now you see it—now you don't. . . . It is the American?"

"Yes. It is because we love each other."

"I have expected this for a long time. And now that it has happened I am not happy."

The little man sighed, and he turned to a little cube of vised steel, at which he had been filing with great tenderness and understanding. He sometimes did work within the limits of a thousandth of an inch.

"I shall miss your cheerfulness and your courage," he said, "but you will come to see us sometimes?"

"Surely. And by and by, when we are settled, you shall take a holiday and come to lunch with us; you and my aunt and the children. We will send a taxicab. You will see for yourselves how happily I am established."

"It will be an event," said her uncle gently.

It would have been far easier for Claire D'Avril

His Daughter

if he had been jocose and cynical. She could better have withstood downright coarseness than sorrow and pity.

"You don't look at me," she said, "and you are so unlike yourself. You aren't angry with me, and yet there is something. . . . I am not an ignorant girl. If, by some blessed chance, I have not till now lived, at least I have seen life. I have seen girls in my station in life go up, and I have seen others go down. Now I, too, have taken a serious step, and one which, for many weeks, I have longed to take. . . . I have begun to live. I am not to be sorrowed over or pitied. . . . I have not taken this great step for the love of finery and of ease, but for the sake of love itself. I have struck no bargain. . . . He is good through and through, like pure gold, and something tells me that I, too, have a good heart. . . . And I cannot bear that you should feel unhappy about me. . . . Why, it's almost as if you thought that I had done something wicked!"

Jules Legros dropped his file among other tools on the bench and opened his arms to her, and they rocked to and fro, sideways, and snuffled loudly as if they had colds in their heads. Presently her uncle released her and wiped his eyes with a corner of his apron.

His Daughter

"I am convinced," he said, "that all is for the best. . . . So get your things together. . . . This bit of metal does not look like much; but its actual importance is of the very first water."

But when she had disappeared into that closet-like room, all bed and bureau, which had been hers for many years, Jules Legros did not at once go on with his filing.

He pulled open a drawer in his work-bench and after ransacking among a thick miscellany of odds and ends, produced a small cylindrical package. It might have been a short length of gun-barrel wrapped in greasy rags. But it was not. It was a stack of twenty-franc gold pieces.

Jules Legros selected one of them with a view to its newness and the clearness of its stamping, and laid it aside. Then he wrapped up the diminished stack in its greasy rags and hid it away in the drawer. He shut the drawer.

He stood in thought, looking now at the one bright gold piece, now at the closed drawer. He reopened the drawer. Once more he unwrapped the gold pieces; he drew out another. . . . Claire D'Avril came out of her old room for the last time. Under each arm she carried a large, bulging pasteboard box tied with string.

"Put down the boxes," said Jules Legros. She did so.

His Daughter

"Shut your eyes, and hold out your hands—palms up."

It was an old game of her childhood. The tears ran down her cheeks.

"Now look."

In each rosy palm she saw a bright gold piece. . . .

"No! No! No!" she cried.

"Silence!" cried her uncle in a terrifying voice, his moustaches bristling.

"But——"

"You have, in truth," he said, "taken a great step. But it was not for the love of finery that you took it, nor for the love of ease. . . . It was for love's sake. Therefore it is not fitting that you should go to him without a little something of your own."

He spoke loudly and with great excitement. He was terribly afraid that at any moment he might regret his generosity and that in his face she might read that regret.

"And furthermore," he thundered, "if you say as much as one single word, why then, to the two gold pieces you already have I will add a third. . . . Kiss me, my poor little fool. . . . And as to the gold pieces, don't tell your aunt!"

So Claire D'Avril departed, weeping, from the

His Daughter

crowded home of her childhood and descended the four flights of stairs, together with the two pasteboard boxes and the two pieces of gold. And she entered the waiting taxi and drove away to her new home.

And she was glad that she was not like some wretched girl of the streets, drawn by the love of finery and of ease. She was an independent girl, going to her lover, because it pleased her to go— a girl free-born and independent—a girl with two pasteboard boxes full of belongings, and with money of her own.

She had, in our money, nearly eight dollars.

Dayton was wrong in thinking that the power to work with real concentration would at once return to him. Mastery and success seemed nebulous affairs. Only Claire mattered.

Another man, having at last come tumbling down from the heights of virtue, might have spent a remorseful morning of regrets and excuses, but Dayton was like a traveller who, in awe and wonder, walks slowly about some beautiful town in a strange land, looking upward. His spirits and his self-respect were not dashed to the ground. They were exalted. It seemed to him that at last he had begun to live and that life was beautiful.

His Daughter

He was in love with Claire. He was sure of that. He did not see how in one man there could be more love for any woman. And it was this fact—the fact of their loving each other—that made all the difference, for love and shame, it seemed to him, can never live under the same roof.

But in spite of his triumphantness and exaltation, it must be confessed that from time to time, while he waited impatiently for Claire to return from her uncle's apartment, he fabricated excuses and offered them to himself for what they were worth. His own was not the only moral collapse (*he* didn't call it that) that he had to think about. He was the captain of his own soul (perhaps), but of that other soul which he had dragged down with him he could never be in command. It was no facility born of experience that had caused Claire D'Avril to yield so easily to him. He had no predecessor on whom the blame could be laid. The innocence with which he had received was no just offset to the innocence with which she had given. We do not, in this connection, speak of a man being ruined (perhaps we should, but we don't); we speak of the girl in the case as having been ruined by the man.

And, like it or not, Dayton was obliged to confess that, from the American point of view at

His Daughter

least, that was precisely the extent of his responsibility to Claire D'Avril. That her innocence had come more than half-way to meet him did not lessen that responsibility one single jot, for the man, himself in love, who takes advantage of a girl's love and passion is only superior, by a pale shadow of morality, to the beast who gains his ends by the use of drugged wine.

Very faintly then he realized that to the labors of making his way in the world he had added, at the very beginning, a heavy weight of responsibility. But, as is usual, he had not gone far enough along the trail to feel the weight of the pack. Indeed, it rested very lightly upon him. It would be long before the straps by which it was suspended began to cut into his shoulders. . . .

Claire D'Avril, swiftly approaching in the taxi-cab with her two pasteboard boxes and her dower of nearly eight dollars, had recovered from the emotion roused by the interview with her uncle. Her face sparkled with happiness. She had the happiness of the lover whose love is returned, and of the schoolboy who, being released from school, is starting on the long vacation. She would not sell any more newspapers; she would sell the rights of the stand to her friend, Mimi Bonheur, who had always coveted them; she

His Daughter

would no longer have to stand first on one foot and then on the other, while detestable men made leering love to her. She was free—beloving and beloved.

Concerning the serious step which she had taken, she had no regret whatever. For a girl in her station of life she had done gloriously well. Her friends would envy her. No one would give her the cold shoulder. Quite the contrary.

In Paris, in certain circles, young people pair off without any sanction of church or law, as freely and merrily as birds. And nobody looks down on these couples any more than anybody looks up to them. And sometimes these trial marriages turn out very well. And some, of course, frivolously and perhaps mischievously undertaken, turn out very badly indeed. Some, sanctioned by faithfulness, suffering, and duration, earn from the community the same respect which is given to the holy state of matrimony. And some actually end in that state.

Claire herself belonged to the wild-goose branch of the human family, and the wild-goose branch, as all men know, is the respectable branch; for wild geese love but once. No justice of the peace, no holy ritual, could have attached Claire more completely or more faithfully to Dayton than her own nature had attached her to him. And when she had flung the door of the studio wide open, she dropped her great boxes and flew into his open arms.

Thus embracing, they conversed for some moments in a very silly, unspellable, and delightful language.

To Claire it was a wonderful home-coming. She made much of it. She said how wonderful it was. Her uncle had never been very demonstrative. The children . . . well, they did fly to her and hug her and kiss her when she came back from work; but this was different. This was so different that she doubted if paradise itself had anything sweeter to offer. . . . Well, be sensible —those were her things, all she had in the world, in these two pasteboard boxes—where should she put them? There was only the one bureau. . . . Suppose she look in the bureau. She did, and found that Dayton had transferred his belongings to the walnut chest of drawers in the studio itself. So she carried her pasteboard boxes into the bedroom and unpacked them on the bed. Hers was a very humble and pitiful wardrobe, with exquisite mendings. It told a story of valor and poverty that brought a lump into Dayton's throat. The more he learned about her the better he liked her.

His Daughter

He watched her tenderly while she stowed her belongings in the bureau drawers. They didn't take up much room. When she had finished, he slid an arm around her and led her back to the studio.

A small kitchen and pantry, which Dayton had not needed, went with the suite; but during Claire's absence he had made an arrangement with the landlord and acquired the use of these important rooms.

"You said you couldn't be really happy if you didn't cook and go to market and wash dishes," he said, "so I've had these rooms put in order, and all we need is a few pots and pans and something to cook. In fact, we've a lot of shopping to do, and I propose that we give the afternoon to it."

Certain phases of that afternoon's shopping embarrassed Dayton. He had planned to remain outside or at a different counter while she bought this and that. But she would not let him off. She would not buy so much as a handkerchief without his direct approval. So he blushed becomingly and, with his thumb and forefinger brought very timidly into use, approved the quality of this white garment or that. He sat in judgment upon stockings and hats, upon dresses and gloves, upon pots and pans and plated knives and forks, and china and table-linen.

His Daughter

And when at last they returned to the studio they had spent several hundred francs and their cab resembled a moving-van. And Claire, although her conscience troubled her because of the fearful sums of money that had been spent, was in a seventh heaven of delight.

When they went to Gibier's for their dinner that night she would have on nothing that was not brand-new—brand-new from top to toe. She was so happy that she could not bear it. Darkness was falling. She flung her arms round Dayton's neck and, closely and tenderly interlaced, they finished the drive home.

She spoiled him frightfully. No doubt of that! The little kitchen she transformed into a scientific laboratory devoted to the fine art of cooking. She had more than her share of the Latin genius. The bright lexicon of her housekeeping did not contain the word "waste." Every day she went to market, a basket on her arm, railed at the market women, browbeat them, beat down their prices and returned with just enough raw supplies, and no more, to furnish forth the delicious meals of the day. And always she brought back with her a few cents' worth of fresh flowers.

Dayton fared exquisitely. Twinges of conscience visited him with less and less frequency, until, the final blunting of his moral sense being accomplished, he accepted his life with Claire as a perfectly satisfactory solution of all the problems to which the flesh and spirit are heir.

Whatever his impulse was, she aided and abetted him. She encouraged him to work, she encouraged him to play, she encouraged him to make love to her. He became peaceful, contented, easily pleased, patient, and hard-working, so that once more he began to make progress in the arts, especially in modelling. Sometimes he thought that he would "chuck everything" and become a sculptor. To model from he had now a very beautiful model and one whose presence in the studio did not embarrass him.

Posing is very hard work; but Claire was a glutton for work, and idleness was hateful to her. So while she posed she knitted, or did the household mending, or embroidered her monogram exquisitely.

They were as happy as two birds in spring. For both of them were good-natured; their impulses were generous, they laughed easily, they were chock-full of vitality, and they were in love with each other. Their loves differed only in the power to endure. Claire would never love another man; Dayton would not always love Claire. But she did not know this, and he didn't. And so it did not in any way disturb their happiness. Neither did satiety cast any shadow over their happiness. It seemed as if they must have drunk at the fountain of eternal youth.

One morning Dayton devoted to casting up his accounts. For two hours he chewed a pencil and made figures on innumerable sheets of paper, and wriggled uncomfortably and mussed his hair. Then he gave a shout of laughter that brought Claire, laughing, from the kitchen.

"Come and sit on my knees," he commanded, "and look at this."

"Well, what is this famous *this?*"

"The details are not for a mere girl to understand. But these are the facts: To have you sitting on my knees, to be inspired by your beauty to do better work, to eat better food than can be bought in the restaurants, to have flowers in the house, contentment, laughter, and love-making, costs me in cold cash just exactly half what it cost me to live miserably alone."

He threw down his accounts and his arms tightened about her.

"Be sensible!"

"I won't!" He grinned at her like a mischiev-

His Daughter

ous schoolboy. "I have declared a holiday. We are to close the studio for a few days and go to Tours where I went to school. And we shall also visit Poictiers and all the wonderful châteaux in Touraine. And I'll sketch and you'll pick flowers. . . ."

And the next day to Tours they went, and from that centre they visited Loches and Chinon and Chenonceaux and Amboise and other great and lordly houses, and spent a day and a night in Poictiers, and Dayton filled a book with sketches, and they lay under trees and looked through the leaves at the sky, and waded in the Loire, and just *didn't* get into a quicksand, and they made love and bought decorative odds and ends for the studio, and on the way back to Paris they stopped off at Blois and there, as luck would have it, as they crossed the court to climb the famous staircase of Francis the First, Dayton saw coming toward them his sister, the Comtesse de Séjour, and a party of friends.

The comtesse took in the situation at a glance, and with the utmost naturalness and good breeding cut her brother dead as a stone. Dayton was thoroughly flustered. Claire looked into his face and had a pang of fear. She could not have said why.

His Daughter

"What's the matter?" she asked.

"Nothing, only that lady is my sister. . . . I . . . do you mind waiting? I really ought to speak to her."

The comtesse heard the sound of his big steps on the pavement, looked over her shoulder, stopped, turned, and with a comical little grimace, waited for him to come up. He bowed over her small gloved hand and kissed it.

"I thought," she said, "that it would be easier for you to be cut. I now understand why you have refused all my sisterly and affectionate invitations to visit us. Let me congratulate you upon your good taste. She's really very pretty and smart."

"She's a brick!" said Dayton simply. "And a great help."

"Of course. But you mustn't abandon your family entirely, or we shall begin to think that the affair is serious. I have had a disquieting letter from Aunt Louise. She says that our mamma is not at all well."

"The last letter I had from mamma she seemed in excellent spirits. . . . It's not serious?"

"Oh, it doesn't seem to be anything that you can put a name to; perhaps it's nothing; but I can't help feeling worried. . . . It's very nice to have had this fleeting glimpse of you. And I hope you will manage to leave Paris for a few days and move about a little in your own *milieu*."

For both Dayton and Claire D'Avril the day was pretty well spoiled; but for the depression which had come over Dayton's spirits he apologized.

"My mother isn't at all well," he said. "That is what depresses me. I can't help feeling that I ought to go home for a while. My sister can't go very well. She has her children and her husband to think of."

"But you—you are free as air!"

"That's not true. And you know it. Every minute that I was away from you would be an age. And of course I'd come back just as soon as I possibly could."

Claire D'Avril's eyes filled with tears, and she uttered a prophecy. She pressed her hand to her heart—hard, as if that organ was hurting her and she wished to repress its beating, and she said: "If you go, you will never come back—to me."

He did his best to comfort her. It was a false alarm, probably. There wasn't one chance in a hundred that he would have to go—not for a long time, anyway. Didn't she know that he loved her? But, for all his assurances and reassurances, they returned to the studio in dismal spirits. Their little heaven could never again be quite the same, for it had established contact with the world.

That night Dayton dreamed that a heavy weight was crushing him to death. He wakened in a quake of fear. And when that had passed, smiled to discover that it was Claire's arm across his chest that had caused his dream. Because of the weight of her arm he could not get to sleep again. He would have moved it, but for the fear of waking her and hurting her feelings. She, in her subconscious mind, was holding him so that he could never get away.

Claire D'Avril cared very little for jewelry; but one day in the Palais Royal she lingered somewhat longingly over a collection of Oriental novelties displayed in the window of a very small shop. The dull solidity of the semiprecious stones in their heavy barbaric settings seemed to exercise a greater appeal to her imagination than the gayer, brighter, and more sparkling gems. In particular, a chain for the neck, set at intervals with scarabs of lapis lazuli, touched her fancy. But when the enamoured Dayton offered to buy it for her, she would not hear of any such extravagance. To be covered, except when one posed, was decent and necessary; but to be foolishly adorned was calling the attention of Providence to oneself; it was inviting criticism.

But the next day Dayton returned secretly to the little shop and bought the necklace. Sunday was her birthday and he intended to make the gift upon that auspicious occasion. In the meanwhile, since the studio had no reserves from Claire, it would be necessary to hide it. He could not leave it with his bankers (it was there that he had disposed, after a day of anxiety lest Claire discover them, of his photographs of Dorothy Grandison), because the bank would not be open on Sunday, and it was with satisfaction that he remembered that one of the tiles in the hearth of the studio's fireplace was loose, and that there was a hollow in the cement beneath.

Claire being safely at work in her kitchen, he lifted the tile, only to find that it had already been made use of as a hiding-place. The tile had been used to conceal a scrap of paper, upon which Claire had written the words: "I love you."

Dayton substituted the necklace for the paper, dropped the tile back into place, and hurried to the kitchen.

His Daughter

Claire was kneading dough. Her back was toward him. The sun was in her hair. Her round forearms were flecked with flour. She looked at him over her shoulder and he craned his head forward and to the left so that he could kiss her on the mouth. Then he showed her the paper.

"When did you write that?" he asked.

"Why," she said, "do you remember that first day, when you brought me in out of the rain?"

"I remember it with shame."

"With shame?"

"I've always thought that, if I'd gone down on my knees and begged ever so prettily and threatened to kill myself if you went away, that you might have stayed. And I should have been spared all those weary weeks of waiting and anxiety and distress."

She laughed a throaty, happy laugh.

"Well," she said, "that day you remember you went for a cab. While you were gone I wrote that and hid it under the tile."

"If I had only found it!"

"It's the only love-letter I ever wrote, and when I wrote it, it didn't mean quite what it would mean now."

"I shall always keep it," said Dayton fervently.

But he didn't always keep it. Neither did he

consciously destroy it or throw it away. It simply disappeared from among his belongings, as such things usually do if they are given time.

On Sunday morning Dayton was the first to wake. The moment Claire, too, had opened her eyes, he bestowed upon her twenty-two great kisses, for that was her age, and a twenty-third to grow on, and then they made their plans for the day.

It was to be a holiday. There should be no going to market, no cooking, not even of breakfast, no dishwashing, no work of any kind. There should be nothing but dressings up, and goings forth, and gayety, and the seeing of sights, and a drive in the Bois for the afternoon, and for the evening a theatre, something that made you put back your head and laugh, and that would have been improper in any language but French.

Like all days devoted entirely to amusement, that day passed slowly; but dusk came at last and they returned to the studio to dress for dinner.

When Claire was dressed, Dayton affected to find fault with her.

"It isn't that your dress isn't pretty and becoming," he said, "but there is something lacking. Just look in the glass; perhaps you'll be able to say what it is."

She looked in the glass; head on one side, head on the other side. With the aid of the hand-glass, she had a look at her profile and her back. And there was nothing wrong that she could see. Indeed, it must be confessed that she found herself rather charming to look at. But because there was some hidden fault to be discovered, she had a puzzled expression which afforded Dayton much gratification. Finally she defended herself.

"There is nothing wrong," she said, "absolutely nothing. The dress is blue, which is your favorite color. It must be a charming dress; you chose it yourself. The stockings are mates. Each hook is in its appointed eye; and except that I am naturally plain, there is nothing the matter with me."

"Yes, there is," said Dayton. "You are a reflection on my generosity. You lack that little something which would make me appear to advantage in the eyes of the world. . . . Look! Hunt! Search! . . . That something exists. It is in the studio, hidden!"

Eager as a child, she rushed into the studio and began to turn things upside down and inside out. Dayton stood at the piano, watched her progress over his shoulder, and heartened or disheartened her by a loud or soft playing of French nursery tunes.

She approached the fireplace. She had looked everywhere. Dayton was playing "Malbrook" *ff*. She dropped to her knees. He switched into "The Marseillaise" *fff*. She lifted the tile. And then she gave a loud cry of joy.

"Oh, the blue necklace," she cried, "to match the blue dress! The beautiful blue necklace!"

In a twinkling she had clasped it about her neck, admired it (and herself) in the mantel mirror, and embraced Dayton so vehemently that he had to brush his hair all over again and retie his tie.

And thereafter, as richer women cling to their pearls, so Claire D'Avril clung to her blue scarabs. Even when she posed for him she would not take the necklace off. She slept in it. Hidden under her plain "Go-to-market dress," it went to market with her. It became her fetich, her talisman. All the other things that he had given her put together had not afforded her so much happiness. She talked to it as if it were alive. She could not have valued a wedding-ring more highly.

Also, from this time on, the hollow under the tile played a regulated part in their lives. They liked to tell each other how much they loved each

His Daughter

other in all possible ways. The hollow under the tile became the regular repository for gifts, for letters:

DAYTON TO CLAIRE

Claire, my well-beloved, when you come back from market I shall be at the paint-shop. I am all out of ultramarine. Each word in this note is a hug, each letter a kiss. If the piano-tuner comes before I return, tell him that middle C sticks like a leech.

CLAIRE TO DAYTON

I don't know where you've gone, my whole world. You have left no word. I have dropped a tear in the pudding. But the Blue Necklace says that there was no time to write; that you left upon a sudden emergency. Soon I shall hear your feet upon the stair. I live to listen.

DAYTON TO CLAIRE

Brightness of Days, I have to go across the river to draw money from the bank and to get my letters. I shall sit by the Marat wastepaper basket to read them. Don't have anything for lunch that has to be served on the minute. I may be a little late. The later I am the more I love you.

CLAIRE TO DAYTON

All my Felicity, I have snatched a moment's time to press my dress and look at my necklace. Next to you I love it most of all my precious possessions. I am the happiest woman in the world.

And so forth and so on.

His Daughter

But sometimes Dayton wrote other letters that were more difficult to write. And there was the occasional letter which, according to their pact, he was allowed (and felt obliged) to write to Dorothy Grandison. But he did not write these letters in the studio. He wrote them on a client's desk in his bank, or on a café table. Claire, it is true, had nothing of suspicion in her generous nature, and would have asked no questions; but still he preferred to keep secret from her the fact that he corresponded regularly with an American girl who was not related to him.

No memory that he had of Dorothy had any longer the power to thrill. He was ashamed of the whole episode. He was ashamed of having cared for her in the first place; of having stopped caring in the second. The thought that she might not have stopped caring, might never stop, sometimes tormented him. He dreaded that inevitable day when he must go through with seeing her again.

In every way Claire D'Avril had still the power to make him happy and contented. If her simple nature could not furnish the infinite variety of a Cleopatra, at least she never allowed their relations to sink to the abased levels of habit. His last kiss would thrill her as his first had. To kiss

His Daughter

him was a wonderful privilege, and not to be exercised in any semidetached mood.

Dayton did not like to face the future. He knew very well that some day he would have to part with Claire D'Avril. What would become of her? He preferred to compromise with his logic, to live in the present, and to pretend that the present was going to last forever.

He was not even in a hurry to see his own country again. Paris could be his own country just as well, for Paris belongs to the whole world. Formerly his idea of success was honors, rewards, praise, money; but his ideas had undergone a change. If he knew that he was doing good work, it was not necessary that any one else should know. If necessary, let the honors, the rewards, and the praise be laid upon his tombstone. Claire D'Avril should always be at hand to keep him physically contented and at peace; he himself, working steadily and with his whole conscience, was well able to take care of his own spiritual comfort. The reward is in the work, not in the accomplishment. They would find somewhere in the country, not far from salt water, an ideal cottage in a grove of old trees. There must be a garden with a high wall, a place warm with sunlight and soft with shade, and there he would paint wonderful pictures of Claire D'Avril, with her gorgeous red hair, her blue eyes, her blue necklace, and her splendid white body dappled with shadows.

And although he knew that these dreams could never come wholly true, he shared them with Claire, and thus did her an injustice. For not only was there in store for her poignant regret of the things that had been, but there would be added still more poignant regret for the things that might have been.

"Listen."

"Do you mean to say you aren't asleep?"

Dayton spoke in a sleepy voice.

"No. I'm thinking."

"What about?"

"Some day you will go away."

"Now, don't start *that*."

"But if you knew that I was going to have . . ."

His sleepiness faded and left Dayton with a clear and startled mind.

"Claire, you don't mean . . ."

"Oh, no. . . . I was only thinking. . . . But there's no such luck."

"I wish you wouldn't think so much. You frightened me. . . ."

"Would it be so very frightful?"

His Daughter

"You don't understand. It . . . it would be out of the question."

Claire did not revert to the subject openly. But it occupied much of her secret thinking. A few days passed and she was hardly able to think of anything else. She had no reason to be afraid of Dayton; but she simply dared not tell him her suspicions.

She made up her mind to confide in her aunt, Madame Legros. For this one, though indolent and in no way admirable, had had considerable experience in the ways of Nature.

"This morning," she said, "do you mind if I go to my uncle's? It is a long time since I have been. I'll be back in time to cook lunch."

"By all means go, if you wish," he said. "But start as soon as possible, so that you will be the sooner back."

With mock seriousness he gave her his blessing, and with genuine feeling a kiss.

A few minutes after she had gone there was a sharp knocking on the door. It was the *concierge's* wife with a cablegram.

Dayton read it, and felt as if his whole life had been knocked galley-west. Only one thought was absolutely clear in his mind. He must get by the shortest road and in the quickest time to the bedside of his dying mother.

His Daughter

He called a taxicab, drove to the office of Thomas Cook, learned that he could catch a fast steamer which touched at Cherbourg; dashed into his bank, turned the remainder of his letter of credit into gold and notes, telegraphed his sister, returned at breakneck speed to the studio, flung his clothes into a trunk, crammed his dress-suit case full of necessaries, paid the rent till the first of the month, waited as long as he dared for Claire, and while he waited, hoping against hope that she would return in time, he wrote her a disjointed, almost inarticulate and grief-stricken letter. Into this letter he stuffed all the money he could possibly spare. At least it would keep her until he returned or could send her more. . . . A moment came, beyond which he dared not postpone his dash for the train. . . . After some hesitation, he did not give the letter for Claire into the keeping of the *concierge's* wife. He did not trust her. Instead, he confided it to the hollow under the loose tile.

He pushed open the door of their bedroom and looked in. The two snow-white pillows seemed to reproach him. A lump rose in his throat and almost strangled him. . . . He fought against tears. . . . It was pitiful, pitiful, that he had to leave her like this—his Claire, his Claire D'Avril, his darling. . . .

His Daughter

The December sky lowered over Paris, dark and grim. A misty rain fell. The streets were greasy; the river, flowing sombrely, seemed to speak of dead things—dead hopes, dead promises, dead virtues. And the sombre, darkly flowing old river seemed, too, to speak of women, unfortunate in love, to whom it had given at the last rest and peace.

Madame Legros had turned her niece's suspicions into certainties.

In all great cities there are men and women who do murder daily for a small fee. Claire D'Avril knew this. And if Dayton insisted, she would go to such a person and make the supreme sacrifice. For love of him she would connive at the murder of her own child. And it amounted to that. For already that child seemed real to her.

Such were her thoughts on descending the four flights of stairs from her aunt's apartment. But in the street the air was fresher, her courage rose, and she began to fight for the continued existence of the child. She would face her lover boldly. She would stand up for her rights; the right of a woman to bear children. Even women who marry for convenience have that right; much stronger, then, is the right of the woman who loves and is faithful.

His Daughter

Already the child seemed real to her—a chubby, adorable, important personage, an arbiter of destinies. In time Dayton would love his child as much as she did; and then—for he was an honorable and loving man—perhaps he would change theirs into a real marriage.

She looked upward, and her thoughts gilded the dark clouds that lowered over Paris. She rested, leaned against a parapet and looked downward on the dark, hurrying river. But the river's message to Claire D'Avril was not an invitation to death. Instead of grim messages, it drew bright pictures for her. She seemed to see a very little child who fished with a very long bamboo pole; she seemed to see a little shaggy dog that went joyously into the water to bring out sticks that the little child had thrown in. . . .

She went on slowly. A man, with the evident intention of scraping an acquaintance with her, drew close and then turned aside as if abashed by the sheer beauty and serenity of her expression.

"At first," she was thinking, "he will not like it; but after a time he will get used to the idea, and soon his tenderness and pity and love will get the better of all other considerations. And then he will be glad, and then suddenly he will

144

His Daughter

take us in his arms and hold us so close—so close that all our three hearts will beat as one."

How should she go about telling him? How best could she disarm him? Oh, he was so tender! She had nothing to fear, and still she was afraid. But he would be just. He would not lay the blame all on her. And, indeed, when it came to that. . . . No. He would assume his full share of responsibility. He would say, as he often said about things that hadn't turned out just as he wished: "No matter. It's happened; it can't be unhappened."

She wondered if he would be entirely depressed by the news; or if he would share in her excitement. She couldn't deny that she was excited and a little rattled. It was wonderful to be turned all at once from an ordinary human being into a miracle. Should she tell him at once? Or should she wait until it was night and she was in his arms? And suppose she did decide to wait until night, could she in the meantime keep her secret? The news surely was in her face. . . .

The plate-glass window of a dark shop reflected her face. She thought: "How big my eyes look!"

Presently she came to the news-stand where she had sold papers to all kinds of people in all kinds of weather. *That* was over, God be blessed!

His Daughter

She stopped to speak with Mimi Bonheur, who now presided.

"How goes it, Mimi?"

"Well enough. And you? Always happy?"

"Always happy."

"You're still together, then! Why, it's a regular marriage! I've seen him. He is very handsome."

"He is very good; and some day he will be a great artist. His color sense isn't good. It's like my ear for music. I can't keep in tune. But you should see the portrait he has made of me in clay. It is so like me that it frightens me."

"So you pose, too?"

"I try to help him in every way that I can."

"Well," said Mimi frankly, "I envy you. You have all the luck. But . . ."

"But what?"

"It can't last forever, you know. You are the same age, or nearly. He will still be young when you are growing old. Take my advice and don't spend *all* the money he gives you. Suppose you returned one day to find your bird flown; and suppose that you had no money, and suppose that you had besides yourself another to provide for."

Mimi Bonheur looked intently into Claire D'Avril's eyes, and broke into a laugh that had

146

in it at once cynicism and friendly feeling. Then she said:

"You have told me nothing; it's a secret if you say so."

Claire D'Avril had blushed hotly.

"But—but I've only just learned myself," she said.

"But — but — but!" Mimi mocked. "The trouble with you is you never studied lying. Your secret is in your eyes. You look like one of the Annunciations in the Louvre. Does he know?"

"I am on my way to tell him."

"He will be furious. But good luck to you!"

"What has happened," said Claire, strong to defend her lover, "is good. He will be glad, just as I am glad."

She came at last to the house in which the studio was, and let herself in with her pass-key.

The wife of the *concierge*, fat, a sloven, stony-eyed, was in the hall.

"Bonjour, Madame Sidon."

"Bonjour, mademoiselle."

"Monsieur est chez lui?"

"Monsieur est sorti."

Claire D'Avril's heart sank, she could not have said why. The stony-eyed Madame Sidon was

His Daughter

looking her over, as a butcher, having sharpened his knife, surveys the body of a calf.

"When did he go out?"

"An hour ago. But don't disturb yourself. *You* can stay."

"Naturally I can stay, madame; but just what do you mean?"

"Oh, nothing. He has paid the rent till the first of the year, and he has put his two trunks on a taxicab and departed in a great hurry."

"It's not true!"

Madame Sidon thrust her massive face close to Claire's. Her face was red with the anger of the habitual liar accused of lying, and her breath smelt of undigested liquor.

"You tell me I lie, do you—you street woman —you dirty girl! Say one more word and I'll bust your face in."

Claire D'Avril did not at once say that word. It was not in vain that she had been brought up in full view of all that goes on in the gutter. She had the knowledge, and the courage, and the physical strength of her class. She was not afraid of Madame Sidon. If it came to blows—very well, let it come to blows. She stood her ground then, and smiled a cold and superior smile.

"Madame Sidon" she said, "too much wine

148

makes too much blood in the head. Any excitement is to be avoided. Exert yourself, fly into a
passion, a vein bursts, and all's over. . . . And
now let me pass. You hate me; but I do not hate
you. I give you good advice. If you are very,
very careful, you may live for a year or two longer.
And listen: while I remain in this house, you
shall treat me with respect. . . ."

She had spoken with a kind of cold and restrained ferocity, which had had the effect of
frightening Madame Sidon almost into that fit of
apoplexy during which she was eventually to suc-
cumb.

Claire D'Avril ran lightly up the stairs, entered
the studio, and closed the door after her. A few
moments later she came to the landing at the head
of the stairs and called to Madame Sidon.

"Did Monsieur Dayton leave no message for
me ?"

"Not one single word, mademoiselle."

"There is a telegram. When did it come ?"

"It was immediately after receiving it that he
began his preparations for departure."

The cable being in English, was Greek to Claire.

She went out, holding the cable in her hand,
and made a tour of the near-by shops, trying to
find some one who knew enough English to trans-

late it for her. But the man who advertised himself as "English Pharmacy" must have referred to the origin of the drugs which he had to sell rather than to his own linguistic abilities, and the shop which displayed in gilt letters "English Spoken Here" had a proprietor who, though he actually did speak several languages (very badly), was unable to read a word in any of them, being stone-blind.

Well, she could cross the river. English really was spoken in most of the big shops. But she did not have to go so far. She saw an old man with a long white beard, who peered through its dirty window at the dirty contents of an antique shop. And she knew that he was an Englishman. And he was too old to be alarmed at being addressed by a pretty girl. He smiled and even wagged his head up and down. His French was almost as bad as his voice was clear and beautiful.

"You must sail at once if you are to reach home in time."

That was what the cable said.

"It's his mother," Claire exclaimed, "she's dying. And so he had to start at once."

The old gentleman wagged his head up and down, and said the French for "Quite so—quite so."

His Daughter

Claire thanked him, and returned to the studio. She moved like a sleep-walker. Why had he gone without leaving any word? There must be a mistake. He wasn't the man to lose his presence of mind, to forget her entirely in the hurry of departure. At least he would see that she had his address, so that she could write to him.

She pressed her forehead against the cold plaster wall, and thought and thought.

There was a knock on the door. It was the *concierge* himself who entered.

"Well, what is it?"

"It is this: that although the rent has been paid until the first of the year, there is a gentleman, an artist, who has had his eye on this suite and who would like to move in at once. I thought that perhaps you and he could come to some agreement that would be advantageous to you both."

"You mean that he would pay me something to vacate at once? Very well. I will think of it."

"He is in the house at this very moment. If you could spare him a moment."

"Very well. Send him to me."

She waited, her back to the fireplace and one foot actually resting on that loose tile in the hearth beneath which was a small fortune in

His Daughter

bank-notes, and better, words of explanation and hope and courage and of faithfulness and love.

The tile creaked under her foot. Was it a message? Was it the warm words beneath demanding to be read, to be taken to her heart? "It is cold here," they may have been saying. "Oh, take us up, take us up, the loving ones, the tender ones. Read us with your great blue eyes. And then, oh, then, lay us beneath the blue necklace against your warm and friendly heart."

But Claire D'Avril heard only an approaching of swift, light feet. She stepped forward and the tile creaked no more.

IV

"I'M not disturbing you?"

Though Claire D'Avril's heart was breaking, she smiled a little and said that he was not disturbing her in the least.

He had a bold, dominating sort of face. He made her think of a condor that she had once seen in the Jardin des Plantes. A bird of prey he looked, and a beast of prey, too; for when he moved it was with the swift-considered grace of a panther, and he was seldom still. His hair, bright and strong-growing, though not a light shade of brown, was in vivid contrast with his black, gayly arched eyebrows and the bright black eyes beneath. He looked at once like a hawk, a panther, and a gambler.

His voice was even, cool as water, and beautifully modulated.

"I am Arnold Charnowski, madame," he said, "and always at your service. Monsieur Sidon has intimated that you may be willing to sublet?"

"As to that—yes," said Claire D'Avril, "on certain conditions."

His Daughter

"That is understood. I may look through the rooms?"

"Of course."

A glance into the kitchen and a glance into the bedroom sufficed him..

"I am satisfied," he said. "And the conditions?"

"There are certain things," she said, "which M. Dayton, who, because of his mother's illness, has had to leave in a great hurry for America, was unable to dispose of—drawings, paintings—that statue—" It was swathed loosely in damp cloths. "You would have to let these things remain until some word concerning them came from him."

"Well," said Arnold Charnowski, "I don't mind. They are workmanlike, if not inspired."

He stepped quickly across to the statue and, in spite of a cry of protest from Claire, boldly removed its swaddling-clothes.

"Aha!" he exclaimed, "yourself!" His bold eyes sought hers.

"He has told the truth?" he asked. "You are like that? Most women, without clothes, are simply ridiculous. But you, you must be simply beautiful."

In Claire's mind resentment and humiliation

His Daughter

fought for the mastery. But Charnowski perceived that he had offended her, and at once changed the subject.

"The utensils in the kitchen—they are yours? The furnishings?"

"The furnishings are Monsieur Dayton's. The utensils I could let you have at a price. I know what each article cost, and after making a proper allowance for wear——"

"I leave all that to you," said Charnowski. "I am not rich, but I do not haggle. Things that I want and am unable to pay for I simply take."

For a quarter of an hour, all Claire D'Avril's business instincts to the fore, they discussed the terms upon which she should vacate the studio. True to his word, Arnold Charnowski did not haggle. He merely said, from time to time: "That is a sum which I am able to pay," and, from time to time, he smiled as if he were enjoying himself. Only once was he at a momentary loss for an answer. She had broken off in the midst of a calculation and suddenly asked him if he was an artist.

"Why, yes—of course," he had answered, and then, his eyes narrowing, had added: "I am a sculptor. And just at the moment I am hunting Paris high and low for a model. You, I suppose, don't pose for every one who comes along?"

His Daughter

"I have never posed for any one but Monsieur Dayton," she said. And a few moments later they had arranged their terms.

"It is understood, then," he said. "You will move out to-day, and I shall move in to-morrow. Monsieur Dayton's possessions will receive the best of care. You will come sometime, I hope, to see how they are getting on? And now let me thank you for all your courtesy." He lifted her hand to his lips. At the door he turned, and came swiftly back to her.

"Madame," he said, "it is only because the matter seems urgent to me that I venture, upon the strength of so short an acquaintance, to make an attempt upon your confidence. The atmosphere of this atelier reeks of tragedy. For God's sake tell me what has happened and if there is anything that I can do to help you."

At that moment he did not look like a bird-beast of prey, but like some impulsive and chivalrous dragon-slayer of the Golden Age. His voice would have charmed away from a child its stick of candy. And before Claire D'Avril knew what she was doing she was telling him the whole story of her relations with Dayton from the beginning to the end. She talked rapidly, swaying slightly, her hands on her hips, her head thrown back. All

His Daughter

these emotions which she had begun to impound at the first news of Dayton's departure found tongue. Her speech became torrential, and as she approached the end of her story there began to mingle with her words a terrible sound of mirthless laughter and of sobbing. She passed, in short, from an extraordinary and touching burst of eloquence into a violent fit of hysterics, during which she tore at her hair and beat her head against the wall.

Arnold Charnowski seized both of her wrists in one hand. He had a terrible grip. The physical pain that it made her suffer brought her to her senses. And she sank exhausted into the big chair.

From the kitchen Charnowski brought a clean cloth dipped in cold water.

"Wash your face," he commanded, "and you'll feel better." She obeyed meekly.

"And now," he said, "listen to me. One fit of hysterics is a good thing. Another might be followed by a disaster. Tragedy, no matter how poignant, must never be allowed to crowd out common sense. The probability is this: that for Dayton, in the hurry of catching his train, it was out of the question to make any provision for you. By this time he has probably written and made

His Daughter

some such provision. You should receive a letter from him to-morrow or the next day. He will enclose money in that letter, and in it he will tell you what you wish to be told. And later, when he has buried his mother, he will return to you. . . . If I am right in these surmises, then it is foolish of you to sob and beat your head against the wall. You might have sprained your reason. . . . Of course, if I am wrong, and the worst comes to the worst. . . . Even if he shouldn't write, even if he shouldn't come back to you . . ."

"He *will* write! He *will* come back!"

"Of course he will; but if, through no fault of his own—accidents will happen—he shouldn't, how much greater than ever would be your need to exercise self-control and to display common sense! You have the three gold pieces that your uncle gave you, and the one hundred and fourteen francs which I am to give you. That is a start. If you are prudent, and can find work which will bring you in something, you will have enough to see you through your time of trial. After that is over, there are a dozen things that you can do to keep yourself going. And let me tell you this: it is written in great letters across the whole of human experience that no pain is great enough to last forever. Even if you have been abandoned, which God forbid, and which I do not for one moment believe, a time will come, as surely as two goes into four twice, when you will once more be profoundly glad to be alive; profoundly glad to love and be loved."

"Never! Never!" cried Claire D'Avril. And again she began to cry; but gently, this time.

He touched her shoulders with his strong fingers.

"If you ever find yourself in need of help or friendship," he said, "I shall be here." His cool voice became wonderfully winning and gentle. "You will look in now and then to tell me how you are getting on?"

"I shall come every day," she said, "to see if there is a letter for me."

And so she did; every day for three long months, but there was no letter. Nor did any letter come for her at her uncle's address; and this was because Dayton, although he remembered the name of the street in which the armorer lived, had never been at any pains to learn or remember his number. And, besides, he considered that the studio was a sufficient address. And so it should have been but for unkind Fate in the repulsive shape of Madame Sidon.

It was she who received and sorted the mail for the whole house. It was she who, though she

dared not open or destroy them, saw to it that
the letters addressed to Mademoiselle Claire
D'Avril were never delivered. And the intervals
between the arrival of such letters became greater
and greater. And May came, and the lilacs
bloomed and the horse-chestnut bloomed, and it
was spring in Paris, and there came no more letters at all.

And Claire D'Avril had long since given up
writing. New York City, Etats-Unis d'Amérique,
was such a very vague address, and it was the
only one she had.

One day she saw Dayton's sister sitting in her
carriage in front of a shop. And she tried to
speak to her and had not the boldness. Madame
la Comtesse de Séjour was in deep mourning.
Claire D'Avril passed close to her victoria, and
the comtesse, though she did not betray the fact
by the twinkle of an eyelash, recognized her, and
felt very cold all over.

"That is Fred's young woman," she thought.
"And what has happened to her is excruciatingly
obvious. The first thing we know she'll be accus-
ing Fred!"

Dayton thought that he was to have the compartment all to himself, and this thought was as

His Daughter

a gleam of pale light in his dark mood; but just before the train started the guard unlocked the door and two women, with a quantity of smart luggage, intruded upon him.

One of the women was obviously the other's maid, and she remained only long enough to lift her mistress's bags into the racks, and then she departed with the guard to be placed in a third-class carriage, as befitted her station in life.

Dayton looked gloomily at the tufted back of the seat opposite. He had not so much as troubled to glance at the lady who was to occupy the compartment with him. At her entrance he had pulled in his feet and made himself small, but he had not looked at her.

She, on the other hand, treated herself to a long, direct look at the handsome American. During this survey the expression of her face underwent no change. Having satisfied her curiosity, she took off her hat, tossed it carelessly to the seat opposite, leaned back and thereafter, for a long quarter of an hour, looked neither to the right nor the left.

You might easily have mistaken them for a pair of lovers who had quarrelled, and who, for the moment, hated each other.

For a while Dayton was not really conscious of

the lady's presence. He was entirely occupied with thoughts of his mother and of Claire. He was only just beginning to realize how much his mother meant to him. It was not until he began to hanker for tobacco that he stole a look at his companion.

Her profile was one in which Flaxman, who designed for Wedgwood, must have delighted. It was as sharply cut as one of their famous cameos; but for the shortness of the upper lip, which betrayed her English nationality, it was a profile purely Greek. That her hair was cut short did not detract from her beauty. It was the blackest hair Dayton had ever seen, strong-growing and sharply curling. It stood well out from her small, well-rounded head, and to another type of face might have given a startled expression. But the effect was not startled—it was startling.

Her dress, severely plain except for a touch of soft white at the throat, was of fawn-colored linen. She was long and slender.

Having looked once, Dayton looked again and again, and was soon drawing deductions. She was English and high-born. She was probably titled. She was undoubtedly celebrated. She was superior to custom and convention. She could be intolerably cutting and insolent. She was a

His Daughter

hard rider, a good shot, very likely, a judge of
dogs and men.

Suddenly, as he was in the act of studying her
profile for the tenth time, she turned and faced
him.

"Do you mind if I smoke?" she asked.

"Of course not. Please do," blurted Dayton.
"And you will too, please, whenever you wish."

"Perhaps you'll let me offer you a cigarette?"
Dayton's case was already in his hand.

"Thanks awfully," she said, "but I'm sure
yours are very bad. Most men's are." She did
not, however, offer him one of her own.

She smoked as if her lungs were made of leather.
He had never seen any one inhale so deeply.
Presently, she spoke again.

"I am going to the States for the first time,"
she said. "Perhaps you can give me good advice."

"I'm sure I can," said Dayton, quite eagerly.
"I've rather prided myself on the excellence of
the advice that I am always able to furnish at a
moment's notice."

The corners of her proud, insolent mouth relaxed. It wasn't a smile, but it was an unguarded
and engaging phenomenon.

"What," he asked, "is the particular axe that
you have to grind in America?"

His Daughter

"Why," she said, "I am going out to make my fortune, for all the world as if I were a younger son."

"Mining—ranching?" Dayton suggested, with a broad smile.

"No," she said, "I am to dance. And perhaps during the process I shall acquire one of your multimillionaires."

"Have you a contract?"

"Oh, yes. Very good, *I* think. Three hundred guineas a week is good, isn't it? I mean for a person who has had no experience in dancing."

"Oh, yes," said Dayton gravely. "Fifteen hundred dollars a week is considered exceptionally good for the inexperienced. But seriously, you don't mean to say that you are not an experienced dancer?"

"Oh," she said, "it's a question of notoriety and figure. You take off as many clothes as you dare. You run with little steps to one corner of the stage and then you appear as if you had suddenly smelled something bad; you turn and run, with shorter and swifter steps, to the other corner of the stage, very purposefully; again the bad smell baffles you, and so on and so forth. Meanwhile, the orchestra plays a Chopin nocturne, the lights are kept very low, you happen to have

164

His Daughter

been born in the English peerage, people whisper
to each other that you are supposed to be the
wickedest woman in London, and come Saturday
night the management is only too happy to hand
you your three hundred guineas."

She spoke with cool insolence and conviction,
as if all these things were matters of common
knowledge.

"Of course," said Dayton, "all that sort of
thing helps, and if you can keep time——"

"I'm rather good at that," she said. "It isn't
as if I'd never even danced round dances. But
the chief element of success, even in dear, wise
old London, is cheek. You'll come to my first
night?"

"Of course."

"Seats one guinea. You shall see me interpret
Chopin."

She laughed a clear, beautiful, and mirthless
laugh.

"You," she said, "are not going to the States
because you want to. I saw you on the platform,
and you looked very sorry for yourself."

"I am going home to see my mother, who is
old and very ill," said Dayton.

"And doubtless you are leaving behind you
some one who is very young and well. But don't

take it to heart. All roads lead back to Paris.
I am tired of turning my head to talk to you.
Come and sit opposite me, unless it makes you
ill to ride backward."

Dayton obeyed smartly.

"I like Americans," said the lady presently.
"And when I saw you put into this compartment
I said to my maid: 'That is my best chance for
amusement during a tedious journey!'"

Dayton tried not to feel pleased and flattered
—and failed.

"I think," he said, smiling, "I ought to point
out to you that I am not one of the multimillionaires."

"Oh," she said, "one is catholic in one's tastes.
One likes one man for his money, another for his
'beaux yeux,' another for his strength. Now, you
are very strong."

"Strong as a lion," said Dayton cheerfully.

"Varsity?" He nodded. She scrutinized him
for some time without speaking. Then she said:

"What's your name?" He told her.

"I am Lady Muriel Strange," she said.

"Oh, but I've heard my sister talk of you—
often," exclaimed Dayton. "She's the Comtesse
de Séjour. She thinks you are the most gifted
and altogether wonderful person in the world."

His Daughter

"She's a good sort, your sister," said Lady Muriel. "But lately one does not meet often. There was a time when your sister threatened to be rather gay and that was followed by a change of heart. She has been led to disapprove of one."

"She says you have a heart of gold."

"And her good husband says that I haven't any heart at all."

"I wish," said Dayton, "that you'd tell *me* the truth?"

She considered this proposal for some moments and then said: "No. I shan't. But I have no objection to your finding out for yourself. You have from here to Cherbourg, from Cherbourg to New York."

"You'll afford me every opportunity?"

"I shan't make any promises."

Dayton did not enjoy the whole trip to Cherbourg. Leaving Claire without seeing her to say good-by had been a hard wrench, and now and then her face, tragic and bewildered, swept between him and the admirable beauty of Lady Muriel Strange. To have left a letter for Claire, and money in the secret letter-box was a satisfaction. It proved that he had done what he could to arrange for everything. And then, of

His Daughter

course, from New York, and from the steamer
for that matter, he would write very often and
with the utmost tenderness. She was more wife
than mistress. He could not have denied that if
he wanted to. After his mother's death (curiously enough, he had no hope of her recovery) he
would return at once to Paris. The meeting with
Claire would more than make up for the enforced
separation.

But, in spite of the gloomy and depressing
thoughts that kept going the rounds in his mind,
Lady Muriel Strange was a wonderfully entertaining experience. To lead the life which she had
led, on nothing a year, men had squandered for-
tunes. She had been deep into dark Africa without any white companion.

She had shot big game in Indo-China and in
India. A maharaja covered with pearls and dia-
monds had offered to dispose of all his other wives,
by drowning if necessary, if she would marry him.
Scandal had not passed her by. Men and women
who knew their London said that in that wicked
city she was the wickedest woman; but when
you looked at that finely chiselled face, contemptuous and ice-cold, you could believe that
she was hard perhaps, hard as marble, but not
that she was wicked. Furthermore, she was re-

His Daughter

ceived at Court, and Scandal, though he clutched at her as she passed, was unable to seize her and drag her in the mud. All this Dayton had heard more than once from his sister. And the more he saw of Lady Muriel the more he believed what his sister had said about her. In Lady Muriel's "golden heart," however, he had no belief. To imagine her stooping to a low action was impossible; and it was impossible to imagine her doing a kind thing in a kind way. He could not imagine her doing a loving, unbending, yielding thing; being in love, for instance, and nestling against the man she loved, and laying her cheek against his.

He hoped that Lady Muriel would not find any friends on the ship, so that he could get to know her really well. She was certainly well worth knowing. She had her imitators, but in all the world there was no one really like her.

But Lady Muriel did find friends on the steamer, and made others, so that from the very start of the voyage he was forced to the conclusion that he would never again know her so well as he had on the long haul to Cherbourg.

Among the things which helped to keep him at a distance was cards. Lady Muriel was a born card-player and an inveterate gambler. Dayton was neither. Furthermore, he could not have afforded to play for the stakes which were affected by the peculiar Englishwoman.

She neither avoided nor encouraged him. She seemed to say: "You had an opportunity to make yourself one of my indispensable friends; you failed to seize it. I am either easily known or not known at all." And so Dayton had plenty of opportunity of thinking of those private troubles from which at one time Lady Muriel had seemed to offer a conspicuous asylum. And in various quiet corners he brooded with genuine sorrow about his mother, remembering little things, comfortings of long ago and wonderful flashes of understanding. Before long he would see that dear face still in death. And he suffered more in anticipation, perhaps, than he was to suffer in fact when that dread and final moment would sweep unfalteringly into his life.

Every day he wrote to Claire a few lines—many pages. It was easy to write to her. It was not necessary to think up things to say. Sometimes he thought that in the course of near events he would very likely see Dorothy Grandison. That thought troubled him a little and left him cold. "I *was* fond of her," he said. "I must have been, but if an angel came down from heaven and told me that I should never see her again it would be rather a relief."

It was the fifth night out. The moon which Dayton, filled with thoughts of Claire D'Avril and longing for her, had been contemplating, had gone under a cloud. The winter air, owing to the nearness of the Gulf Stream, was sticky, warm, and muggy. A light overcoat was too much; no overcoat at all, unless you kept moving, was not enough. So Dayton made the round of the deck. Lady Muriel and Drummond, the American millionaire, were among the few who still occupied steamer chairs. It was eleven o'clock.

Lady Muriel, reclining at ease, was in deep shadow. Drummond, bending forward, his elbows on his knees, was engrossed with her. She was making him laugh. Dayton caught the cool tones of her voice as he passed. They had not noticed him. Anger found place in his heart. She must have seen him, she might in common decency have said a word of recognition. She had not spoken to him all day. What a cold-blooded proposition she was!

After that he kept to the starboard side. For half an hour he walked briskly, trying to brush the gloomy and peevish thoughts from his mind. The starboard was also the windward side of the

His Daughter

ship. This annoyed him. Who was Lady Muriel Strange that she should keep him from the shelter of the deck-house?

Suddenly, in the light of a smoking-room port-hole, he met Drummond face to face. Drummond also looked extremely cross and peevish. They wished each other a curt good night. Drummond disappeared into the smoking-room and Dayton crossed to the shelter of the port deck. From having seen Drummond he inferred that Lady Muriel could be no longer making her shad-owed corner fascinating. But he was mistaken. She had not moved, and she called to him.

"Come and talk to me," she said.

A moment later Dayton, completely mollified, bending forward, elbows on knees, was sitting where Drummond had sat.

"I have sent Drummond to bed," said Lady Muriel; "he is an impossible person. He is one of the few men that I have known whom I couldn't ever learn to love for his money alone."

Dayton chuckled. He did not admire either Drummond or his money.

"Sometimes," said Lady Muriel, "I rather fancy that I have no heart. What do you think? You were to study me, you know, and render an expert opinion."

His Daughter

"My opportunities for studying that question have been rather limited," said Dayton.

"Yes, I know. I suppose I've seemed rather horrid; but you don't play cards. Tell me . . ."

She did not at once ask the question that she had in mind. His eyes, now accustomed to the darkness of Lady Muriel's corner, seemed to discover in her eyes an altogether new and trembling brightness.

"I'll tell you anything," he said.

"Do men like you?" she asked abruptly.

It was the last question that Dayton could have anticipated. Its unexpectedness brought a stammer into his answer.

"Why—I—I—don't know. I hope so."

"You see, women *do* like you. And so often the two things don't go together."

"How do you know that women like me? I don't know that they do. I wish they did."

She laughed very softly. "Give me your hand."

"Going to tell my fortune—" he broke short off, almost in horror. She had seized his hand with a kind of ferocity, and with both hers was pressing it to her heart.

"Now do you know if I've got a heart or not?"

He could feel it beating furiously, but he did not answer her question.

173

His Daughter

"Don't be a fool," she said, the words all hurried and huddled together. "Kiss me!"

When they met for the first time next day, in the presence of Drummond and some others, it might have been thought that Lady Muriel Strange had for Dayton a feeling amounting to aversion. And if, at the end of the voyage, the passengers had been asked to state which man of all those who had been attentive to her had most interested the famous Englishwoman, no passenger would have named Dayton.

Cautious in the open, almost to the point of absurdity, she was, under the rose, a creature all passion and daring. She did not care what she said or what she wrote. No deck-steward carried Dayton *two* letters from her, but during the remaining short days of the voyage every available deck-steward carried him one. And these letters, Dayton at the earliest opportunity tore into tiny fragments and consigned to the ocean piece by piece. They terrified him and they humiliated him. And yet he regretted that he dared not keep them.

For his own conduct he made excuses, thereby proving that of that conduct he was ashamed. The intrigue was not of his seeking. It was she

His Daughter

who had made love to him.   As for Claire D'Avril
—well, she was not his wife, was she?

But Dayton could not swallow his own excuses.
He loved Claire, and he had been faithless to her
even while he was busy grieving over their separation and longing for her.   He did not love Lady
Muriel; and yet, if she wished it, he felt that he
would have to marry her.   What would Claire
think of him then, poor thing?   And what would
his life be with such a woman as Lady Muriel for
his wife?   How long would her sudden infatuation for him last?   How soon would a sudden infatuation for some one else begin?

He was plunged into depths of remorse from
which no excuses which he was able to make could
float him.   Nor was it any great satisfaction to
imagine that women were more necessary to him
than to other men and to place the blame on
Fate.

"But you don't care for me the way I care for
you."

"But truly—look for yourself.   I'll turn out the
light."   There emerged from the darkness a circular patch only less dark.

"You see now.   It's not as dark as it was.   For
your own sake tell me to go."

His Daughter

"It's been like that for hours; it's only four o'clock. There's so much to be talked over. There'll be neither time to-morrow nor opportunity. We must arrange how we are to meet and where. And there's one thing you've never said. Oh, you know jolly well how to hold your tongue . . ."

"What haven't I said?"

"You haven't said that you love me."

"But I do—don't I?"

"Turn on the light. . . . Now look me in the eyes and say it." After a moment's hesitation he said it; but she sighed.

"It's no good," she said "you *don't*."

"Nor you," he answered. "You don't love me."

"I wonder."

"I don't."

"If you loved me . . . Oh, what is the use? What is the use of anything? . . . And so I don't love you, my handsome young man! Aren't you the fine one to be telling me that—*considering*. Well, then, I *don't* love you; but listen. . . . If you went out of that door, and it closed behind you, and a dark angel told me that I should never see you again, I'd manage to squeeze myself through that port-hole and drop into the ocean and drown."

"I think that you think you love me."

His Daughter

"A lot of thinking I've done. You turned my blood into fire, and my self-respect—even I have that, you know—every woman has—burnt to the ground."

Dayton drew a long breath, and then spoke with a voice which he strove to make even and sincere.

"Listen, dear," he said; "there's one thing we haven't decided, and that's when we are to be married."

She was silent for what seemed to him a long and ominous interval. Then——

"I'll always be glad to remember that you said that," she said. "And I believe that you'd go through with it. Though you are slow at cards, and don't like to take sporting chances, you're a thoroughbred, you are. . . . But I'm only one kind of bad. I'd sooner be dragged through hades by the heels than marry a man who didn't love me. . . . You don't mean to go through life hurting people, but you are the kind of man— well, every millionth man is born like that—I don't know what the quality is—perhaps a liquid gleam in the eye—perhaps something that has neither name nor tangibility—but think over the story of your whole young life and see if I'm not right. . . . Very few women will ever say 'No' to you. That, my dear, is your great gift from

His Daughter

the gods. You are just beginning to find it out.
. . . You can twist us round your fingers. . . ."

"Then marry me."

"No."

"*Please!*" She shook her head.

"I can't twist *you* round my fingers, that's certain," he said. "And so you see I don't believe in the great gift from the gods. If I did I'd shoot myself. I want to be just ordinary—and decent."

She laughed a strange, harsh little laugh. "It's for you to choose. And if you make a hack of your life, don't say I didn't warn you. Some day you'll love some one, but she'll be neither your mother nor your wife nor your mistress, and she'll make you wish that you'd never been born."

"Neither mother, wife, nor mistress!"

"Remember that."

"But who, then?"

"Oh, you'll know when the time comes. And now please go. It's getting frightfully light . . ."

"You'll let me know when I can see you in New York?"

"Of course. Now run along and try to get your beauty-sleep."

The doctors told Dayton that his mother could not last very long. For the moment she was

178

His Daughter

comfortable. The attacks came usually at night.
There was no pain less bearable. . . . But if in
the beginning the growth had been cut away?
. . . It had been, only to recur in another place;
there had been more cutting. The disease was in
her blood; sooner or later it must tap an artery;
then the end would come drowsily and peacefully.
It was not until her condition could no longer be
concealed that she had told her children. She
had been extraordinarily brave. Even when the
attacks were on she didn't make much fuss. . . .
But how long? . . . Oh, she might go on resist-
ing another six weeks, or—there was no use minc-
ing matters—she might die within twenty-four
hours. Could he see her now? Oh, yes; certainly.

He hurried up the well-remembered stairs to
the well-remembered room. But in the narrow
brass bed, propped up with pillows, was not the
suffering wreck of humanity which he had been
led to expect. Mrs. Dayton looked very natural.
She was neither emaciated nor colorless. And, although her voice trembled, it was with the joy of
seeing her son after their long parting. But when
he would have taken her in his arms she restrained
him with a quick gesture.

"Your old mother has to be handled with
gloves," she explained.

His Daughter

"But you look so well, so like yourself!"

"How I look doesn't matter; but come the other side, so that the light will be in your face. I want to see how *you* look."

"Well?"

"You've changed," she said critically. "You are no longer collegiate. You look authoritative. You look as if you could get things done. . . . What an enormous beautiful son it is!"

"If you'd only told me, you know, don't you, that I would have come home at once?"

"Of course I knew, but now that you are home, I want you to go your own way, see your friends and all. I couldn't bear that you should just wait about the house. Be in and out, and never far off. That's what I want. It may be a long wait. I will make it as long as I can. I don't want to die. I prefer life, on almost any terms, to death. . . . They've told you, I suppose, that there is absolutely nothing to be done?"

"You've tried radium?"

"Everything. I've fought it hard from the beginning, and burned money. You mustn't hold that against me. . . . You look a little tired. Was it a hard trip?"

"It seemed very long at times."

"Of course it did. You were anxious about

your mother. I see by the paper that you had distinguished fellow passengers. Aren't the papers wonderful! I read all about your trip before you were able to get up-town from the wharf. I must know what *you* thought of Lady Muriel. I've heard so much about her. It seems that she is coming over to dance. You met her, of course?"

"We came up from Paris in the same compartment," said Dayton, "and scraped an acquaintance. She is very interesting, very distinguished. She is always very good-looking; and there are times when she is really beautiful. But, as to the dancing, I'm sure I don't know."

He was astonished at the ease and nonchalance with which, in his mother's presence, he had appraised Lady Muriel. It wasn't true, the old notion, that he could hide nothing from his mother. When she had brought up Lady Muriel's name he had had a sort of sinking feeling; he had feared that somehow or other, with every opposite wish and intention, he would manage to give Lady Muriel away and himself too.

The ordeal was over and his mother passed to other topics. A quarter of an hour later she dismissed him. She had to rest, she said. He could come to see her again at seven, for a few minutes, before he dressed for dinner. Of course he could dine at home, but wouldn't it be more cheerful for him at his club or a restaurant?

But for several days Dayton took all his meals at home. Then, more by his mother's insistence than his own volition, he began to go about a little; but he was very attentive, very dutiful. He was in and out of the house all day. Lady Muriel seemed to have dropped out of his life. Whenever he called at her hotel she was out. He was not sorry. Now that time had lent a little perspective, it was to the gentleness and naturalness and sanity of Claire D'Avril's affection that his thoughts turned more often than to the fire of Lady Muriel's. If Claire could have known precisely what went on in his mind she would very likely have forgiven his infidelity.

But one morning he received a note from Lady Muriel:

I've tried to go my way, and let you go yours, but it's no good. If you came to see me this afternoon at five I'd be in.

He passed the day in a kind of subdued excitement. It astounded him to discover how strong a hold Lady Muriel had on him. And he went for some hours without once thinking of Claire D'Avril. Just as he was about to leave the house

His Daughter

the postman brought a special-delivery letter for him.   He ripped it open and read:

DEAR FRED:
  We've only just learned that you are in town.   We are in town too for the night at the Royal.   Dorothy is beside herself at the idea of seeing you.   Of course it isn't in the compact, but you've been so very, very good, both of you, that I haven't the heart not to make just one exception.   So won't you dine with us to-night at 7.15, and go to the play afterward?
                                    MARY GRANDISON.

He put off answering until he had reached Lady Muriel's hotel.   Then, after he had sent up his card, leaning over the long office desk, his heart beating in a heavy, disconcerting way, but not at thoughts of Dorothy, he wrote:

DEAR MRS. GRANDISON:
  With the greatest pleasure, if I may make the acceptance conditional upon my mother's wishes.   She is very ill indeed.   But the moment I get back to the house I will telephone and be definite.   Please forgive this scrawl.
  With admiration, always,
                                    FREDERICK DAYTON.

"May I come in, mother?"
"Of course."
"I've been invited to dine and go to the play

with some old friends. I ought to go if I can. Would you mind?"

"Of course not, dear. But if you are to go to the play, dinner will be in the earlies, and it's now quarter of seven."

"Dinner is for quarter past. But I can bathe and dress in eight minutes when my things are laid out. I was timed once on a bet. May I use your telephone?"

Presently he was speaking with Dorothy Grandison and telling her that he would come with pleasure.

"What a pretty voice she has, dear."

"You could hear? Yes. Hasn't she? And she's a mighty pretty girl. Only a kid, you know; but we got to be great friends in Egypt and afterward in Paris. She and her mother and I."

"I know—you wrote me about them. I thought at one time—but then you mentioned them less and less, and finally not at all. I thought at one time that there might be something between you."

"Why," said Dayton casually, "how could there have been? She was only fifteen or sixteen."

"I'm sure from her voice that she is good and wholesome."

"She's a perfect little dear, and so is her mother."

His Daughter

"I wish," said Mrs. Dayton quietly, "that I could see you settled before I go."

"Please, please don't talk about going, mumsey."

His mother smiled brightly.

"Well, if *you* don't hurry and go, *you'll* be late."

He dressed savagely.

"How," he said, "can I go straight from Muriel to a woman like my mother, and talk as if butter wouldn't melt in my mouth, and then on to Dorothy and sooner or later back to Muriel?

"If my mother knew, she'd despise me, and if the Grandisons knew, they'd simply pass me up —and I take the risks, and it doesn't even worry me. . . . I used to think I was a decent lot . . ."

He glanced at himself in the glass and said:

"I'm beginning to hate you."

Fifteen minutes later he made an end of that beginning. Mrs. Grandison had tactfully delayed the last touches to her toilet, so that Dorothy could have a minute alone with him.

That pure, beautiful, and faithful face, only dimly remembered, came back into his life as simply as it had gone out of it. He had only time to observe that she was older, that she was really grown up now, and that her eyes were blazing with happiness.

His Daughter

He had wondered how he should get through with that meeting. He wondered no longer. He simply took her in his arms and kissed her, and distinctly he heard himself murmur:

"It's been so long—so-o long!" It was then that he really hated himself.

V

BUT during the evening Dayton's sudden self-hatred petered out. Aware of the happiness which the mere sight of him afforded Dorothy, he could not continue to hate himself. For the fact that for many months now he had thought of her with coolness, shamefacedness, and perhaps remorse, he had no good excuse to offer. He was the kind of man, it seems, whose heart is not made fonder by separation. That was his misfortune, not his fault. He was sorry; but he could not help himself. It was something at least to find that there had been a genuine quality in his sentiment for Dorothy. That sentiment had not died—it had merely been asleep; and now behold it was awake, its wide eyes filled with peacefulness and pleasure.

They dined and they went to the play. They laughed like children and Mrs. Grandison's motherly heart went out to them. It would be nonsense, she thought, to insist on any longer interval of probation; her mind could pick no flaw in their love for each other. Bless them, she thought, they've written only the most casual and occa-

sional letters and they've kept their compact with
the utmost punctiliousness, and all the time they
were eating their hearts out for the sight and
sound of each other. There is no reason why
they should not be openly engaged, and in a year
or so—of course Dorothy will be much too young
even *then*, but still, etc., etc.

It had always been in the back of Dayton's
thoughts that if, when she was grown up, Dorothy still cared for him, he would chivalrously pretend that he still cared for her and they would
be married. And she would never know the sacrifice he had made. She would never know. He
would play the lover to the end.

But now it was in the forefront of his thoughts
that she was grown up, and that she still did care
for him, and always would, and that marriage
with her would entail no sacrifices upon his part
—none whatever. Indeed, he was rapidly falling
in love with the idea of that marriage.

"No, I mustn't come up. It's the longest I've
been away from my mother since I got back. It's
been splendid. I've loved every minute of it.
Are you *really* going back to the country to-morrow ?"

"Yes. *Really!* But you must come to see us.
We're only an hour from town."

His Daughter

"Really! I may really come?"

"You've been very good children," said Mrs. Grandison. "If you want to see each other I shan't interfere."

A heavenly light came into Dorothy's eyes. It seemed to her that she was listening to celestial music. And in that moment Dayton knew that irrevocably, unless death intervened, he and Dorothy would one day be man and wife. He looked very proud and manly, and a fine note of seriousness came into his voice, for during those moments he had made many high resolves.

"May I tell my mother," he asked, "and take Dorothy to see her?"

"Oh," cried Dorothy, "I'm afraid she'll just look at me and know I'm not good enough." Dayton laughed softly.

"When she looks at you," he said, "she will be so proud and happy that she will forget all that she has suffered."

"There is another important person to be told," said Mrs. Grandison. "Dorothy's father knows nothing about you young people. Nothing whatever."

"He must know from me, then," said Dayton.

"I wish I could be behind the door when you tell him," said Dorothy.

His Daughter

"Is he a violent, dangerous man?"

Then they all three laughed as if Dayton had said something very funny indeed. And upon that laugh, at the door of the elevator shaft, he bade them good night.

He ran ever so lightly up the stairs to his mother's door, but she heard him and called out that she was awake.

"I had my nap this afternoon," she explained. "Were the Grandisons as nice as ever?"

"Even nicer," said Dayton. He drew a chair close to the bed and took one of his mother's hands in both his. The expression on his face was one of sweetness with gayety. To his mother he seemed an adorable boy—frank, high-minded, sweet-tempered, gentle, wise beyond his years, beautiful to the eye, and tremendously talented.

"Mother," he said, "at our last interview, brief though it was, you expressed a wish to see me settled. Has it ever occurred to you that I am the most dutiful son in the world and that your wish is ever my law?"

A look, part pleased, part anxious, came into Mrs. Dayton's eyes.

"Darling!" she exclaimed, "what are you going to tell me?"

His Daughter

"I am going to marry Miss Grandison, mother."

"Oh, my dear!"

"She is beautiful, mother, and sweet, and good, and loyal. I'm not worthy to kiss the dust on her little shoes."

"This is a great shock to me," said Mrs. Dayton, "a great shock."

"But, mother, you said——"

"I know I *said*. I was theorizing. But this young lady seems to be a fact."

"But when I *tell* you——"

"Did any mother ever believe what her son told her about a lady she had never seen? Of course not; it would be inhuman. When you tell me that she is good and that she is loyal, I believe that you think so. Of course you do. You are in love with her. But I am not in love with her. . . . Not yet. I should see her with unbiassed eyes."

"You shall, dear; just as soon as it can be arranged. They live out of town."

"I know who they are—vaguely. They are the right sort of people——"

"I thought I was the bearer of good news. Instead I'll have given you a bad night. I'm *so* sorry. I'm so hot-headed and impetuous. I *might* have waited till morning."

His Daughter

"I wouldn't have had you wait. But tell me
—when, how long——?"

"Ever since Egypt, mother dear. But she was
so young that her mother put us on a sort of probation; which was just and wise; and now, if her
father doesn't find fault with me, all is well."

"I'd just like to see him find fault with
you!"

"Did it ever occur to you, mother, that the
father of a daughter has a great deal in common
with the mother of a son?"

"What nonsense you do talk! . . . And now
I think I'd rather you kissed me good night. This
has all been very sudden and very bewildering."

"I'm only worried about your state of mind till
you've seen her," said Dayton. "After that I
shall have no worry of that kind. . . . Good
night, mother dear, and bless you."

Mrs. Dayton did not sleep at all and Dayton
did not sleep well. It was not enough, it seems,
that for the first time in many years he knelt by
his bed and prayed to God to make him a good
man. He had no sooner dropped his head on the
pillow than it began to fill with troubling thoughts.
It is not necessary to go very deeply into those
thoughts. It is enough perhaps to record that
more than once during the night he exclaimed:

His Daughter

"O Christ! If only I'd known *then* what I know now!"

It was not the thoughts of his conduct with Claire that tortured him, but those concerning Lady Muriel Strange. It seemed incredible that a man of his breeding and ideals should go direct from a base and transient intrigue to engage himself to a girl purer than snowdrops, innocent and utterly trusting.

"Well," he thought at last, "it's ugly—unforgivably ugly. But nothing like that shall ever happen again. And though Dorothy will never know that anything like that ever did happen, I'll make it up to her, so help me!—I'll be so good to her that some day, perhaps, I'll forgive myself."

But he could not sleep. There was the interview with Dorothy's father to be gone through with; there would have to be another—a very final interview, indeed—with Lady Muriel; and then, of course, he must make some sort of arrangement about Claire D'Avril. She must never be allowed to want for anything.

But he did not look as if he had had a bad night when he stepped into the tall building in Exchange Place where Mr. Grandison had his offices. A cold bath and a brisk walk part of the way down-town had brought back the color to

His Daughter

his cheeks and the sparkle to his eyes. Nor did the perplexities of his life trouble him as much in the bright sunshine as they had in the dark.

Mr. Grandison, recently appointed receiver for a traction company that was not paying dividends or anything else to speak of, was a very busy man and an important man. Therefore he could not afford to put on airs and feign inaccessibility. Though not a great man, he was just as accessible as if he had been. And he had no sooner received Dayton's card than he gave the order for Dayton to be shown into his private office.

"I am delighted to see you at last," he said. "Your name is very familiar to me. To certain members of my family you are one of the great enthusiasms. Sit down. There are cigarettes in that box. Have you come to see me on business or pleasure?"

"I won't deny that it's a pleasure to see you," said Dayton, and he found it so difficult to say anything else that he began to blush and feel very nervous.

"I'm afraid I'm going to give you a shock," he said presently. "I've asked Dorothy to marry me, and she says she will."

Mr. Grandison sighed, frankly and openly, and said: "Oh, dear me!"

His Daughter

And at once the lines in his face, dug by care and responsibility, seemed to darken and deepen. Still, a smile flickered in one corner of his mouth.

"That is a shock," he said, "which the flesh of all male parents is heir to . . . but Dorothy, Mr. Dayton, is much too young to think of marriage."

"I know she is," said Dayton, "but all the same she is thinking about it. We've been thinking about it ever since we were in Egypt. So it isn't as if we weren't sure of our sentiments, is it?"

"Can you support a wife?"

Dayton did not like to say that his mother was on her death-bed and that from her he would inherit an income sufficient for two persons whose wants did not run to yachts. Neither did he like to confess that he himself had yet to earn his first cent. So he said:

"I've had a good training, Mr. Grandison; I'm naturally a hard worker, and if the worst comes to the worst there's a certain amount of money back of me. Supporting Dorothy is the least thing that worries me."

"And there are great things that worry you?"

"Yes, sir. Unworthiness is the great thing. I have done things that I wish to heaven I hadn't done. But there's nothing with a string to it;

nothing that can come up out of a clear sky to hurt Dorothy."

And he thought he was speaking the truth; for he had no inkling that a seed of his sowing had sprouted in the dark and that he had given a hostage to fortune.

Mr. Grandison again sighed with frankness and openness.

"Have you spoken to your own people?" he asked presently.

"I've told my mother," said Dayton. "My father isn't living."

"And doesn't she think *you* are a little young?"

Dayton smiled. "She won't approve at all until she knows Dorothy. And I've come to you, sir, among other things, to ask if I may take Dorothy to see my mother. My poor mother is a very sick woman——"

"I am concerned to hear that."

Dayton explained a little.

"—so she can't possibly get well, and she's troubled about me, and it will be such a comfort to her to see Dorothy and to learn for herself into what good keeping I want to give my life."

"Dorothy," said Mr. Grandison, "has always done pretty much as she pleased. It's not that we were ever slack with her, but that she was just

His Daughter

naturally one of those children who always seem to be on the track of doing the right thing. If she has set her heart on you, Mr. Dayton, I can only say, please wait until she is a little older, and then, if you still feel the same way about each other, why, the affair may legitimately be called your own and no one else's. Don't misunderstand me when I say that I am sorry that she has fixed her affections so early in life. It would have been more satisfactory to know that she had looked about a little before making her choice. However"—and here he smiled in a really friendly way, and held out his hand—"I have always had faith in my little daughter's judgment."

Dayton gripped the extended hand hard.

"I'll try to be a good son to you," he said, and a moment later, since neither appeared able to think up anything further appropriate to the subject, the weighty interview somewhat lamely terminated.

"My dear," said his mother, when he had kissed her, "I've had a visitor."

"Not Dorothy?"

"She had just a moment before catching her train."

Dayton was smiling broadly. "And now you

His Daughter

believe some of the things a son tells a mother about his best girl."

"I think," said Mrs. Dayton, "that she has the sweetest and purest mind of any girl I ever knew. I can't tell *you* how happy I feel this morning; how very happy!"

"She never even told *me* that she was coming."

"She said she came on impulse, that she couldn't help coming. She brought me those beautiful violets. And I gave her a little picture of you when you were a baby—the one with the big gloves. My dear, my heart tells me that you have found a treasure; and then she is so very lovely to the eye."

"I'm so glad that you are glad."

"It was worth a bad night."

"You had a bad night?"

"No pain. Just sleeplessness."

Mrs. Dayton was to have another bad night—not "just sleeplessness," but a night of pain leading by degrees into agony. But Dayton was not called; she would not let them call him. And indeed, when she knew that presently the pain would be greater than she could bear in silence, she made them shut her door and hang a heavy curtain over it so that those cries and exclamations which she had no longer the power to repress

His Daughter

should not disturb his sleep. He slept like a top, and in the morning, before he was even out of bed, received a note from Lady Muriel containing the simple but expressive words: "Five o'clock."

Well, he would have to go. He couldn't very well break off with Lady Muriel by letter. He had offered to marry her and she had refused him. He would tell her gently but firmly that henceforth they must be strangers. It was very easy to lie in bed and say his say; but as five o'clock approached he became distinctly nervous and apprehensive. He admired his new armor of righteousness and thought well of it; but he had yet to prove it in the field.

And he had no sooner stepped into Lady Muriel's sitting-room than Lady Muriel made a distinct dent in that armor. For she murmured something about "at last," and laced her arms tightly about him and pressed her mouth to his.

Dayton's armor of righteousness suffered a frightful dent in this assault. His heart began to beat furiously, and to appear cool and self-possessed caused him the greatest effort that he had ever made in his life. But somehow or other he managed not to return her embrace and not to return her kiss. And so it was that the new armor of righteousness was not pierced, but only greatly dented.

Lady Muriel's arms dropped to her sides, and she backed slowly away from him.

"For goodness' sake," she said, "what is the matter with you?"

"I've come," Dayton faltered, "to say—to tell you——"

"I didn't suppose you came to tell the rug or the fire-dogs—so look at *me*."

Dayton looked at her but could say nothing.

"Well—out with it—who is she?"

"She's the girl I'm going to marry," said Dayton very quietly. And so——"

"But day before yesterday you were here with me in this—no, not in this room."

"I know," said Dayton.

She laughed harshly.

"And you said," said she, "that in my arms——"

"I know what I said."

"But you didn't mean it."

"I suppose I meant it when I said it."

"You said that even death would be sweet—and then you run around the corner and, such is the illimitable nature of your amorousness, engage yourself to be married. . . . Is the mar-

His Daughter

riage absolutely necessary? Surely a man like
you . . ."

"Please don't," said Dayton. "The abuse that
I deserve is so obvious that it doesn't seem worth
while to go into details. There is nothing that
you can say to me that I haven't said to myself."

She came closer to him.

"You've got a holier-than-thou expression at
this moment which tickles my risibles. . . .
You're not going to be faithful to this lady after
marriage. If you don't know that, you're a fool."

The telephone at this moment rang sharply.
Lady Muriel placed the receiver at her ear.

"Who? Mr. Drummond? Hold the wire. . . ."
She covered the mouthpiece of the telephone with
one hand and, turning to Dayton, said quietly:

"What shall I say, Fred?"

"I'm going in just a moment, Muriel."

"Right-o!" She turned and spoke into the
receiver. "I am at home. You may show him
up."

"I know you despise me—" Dayton began
humbly.

She shrugged her shoulders.

"I've never yet cried over spilt milk," she said.
She drew a deep breath. Then she smiled.

"You're afraid of me, aren't you?" she said,

"afraid that I'll play the bad fairy in your new happiness? I shan't. I've got a certain sense of justice. You did offer to marry me, and I refused. If I don't want you to belong to somebody else I have only myself to blame. Do you know why I refused to marry you? No, you don't. I'll tell you now. I refused to marry you because I am a bad egg and because I love you. If you think I am just a sly woman of ungovernable passions you are wrong. My love for you is greater than my passion. That is why I shall say goodby to you calmly and not cut my throat after you've gone. I'd rather be boiled in oil than hurt you in any way. Only your own mother can say that much. You'll get no such love from the girl you are going to marry. You'll not be faithful to that girl; you are too attractive to women and you've got altogether too much temperament. But the shadow that eventually comes into your young lives will not be Muriel Strange. . . . And now, dear boy, because I'm so very sorry for myself, put your arms around me and kiss me good-by."

He kissed her, oddly enough, with a kind of awe and reverence, and at that moment Drummond, the millionaire, knocked upon the door.

"Ah," said Lady Muriel, "I'm so relieved you've

His Daughter

come. Poor, dear Dayton was beginning to bore me."

Drummond's small eyes brightened with unalloyed pleasure. And, the door having closed upon Dayton, he proceeded at once, and for the hundredth time, to lay his millions at Lady Muriel's feet. This time Lady Muriel was very decided with him.

"Drummond," she said, "you've made that offer once too often. I accept. And the consequences are on your own head."

"Good!" cried Drummond in an ecstasy; "and I was beginning to think you cared for that Dayton fellow."

"I hope you don't think I'm beginning to care for you, do you?"

Drummond fairly roared with laughter. "What a woman you are!" he exclaimed.

Gradually Dayton began to do a little work. Owing to his mother's condition he did not rent a studio, but carried his paraphernalia into a north-lighted attic room in his mother's house. Here for several hours a day he modelled, drew, or designed as the spirit moved him. He made busts of his mother's nurses; of the cook who had come into the family the year he was born. And he

drew and colored many designs for gardens and
garden furniture—benches, fountains, and sun-
dials.

One thing greatly troubled him—Claire's silence.
Some of his many letters must have reached her.
He felt sure of that. Why, then, did she send
him no word? That something serious might
have happened to her, that her life even might
have been snuffed out, never occurred to him.
To the young the possibility of death is not be-
lievable. Nor did it occur to him that in her distress at finding him gone she might have failed to
look under the loose tile in the hearth.

Finally, always addressing her at the studio, he
wrote her as tenderly and gently as he could, tell·
ing her a fact that for some time now she must
have gathered from his letters (if she had received
them). He wrote her that he was going to be
married. But he said he felt it his privilege to
provide for her future, and he named a sum of
money which he proposed to forward as soon as
he should receive an address at which the draft
would surely find her.

He did not write this letter until May. And
not until it was written did he feel that his life
was no longer complicated by Claire D'Avril. He
had been unsparing in his efforts to locate her and

His Daughter

to be as kind to her as his circumstances warranted. And if he could not explain her silence, it was at least one of the facts of existence—for which he saw no reason to blame himself.

Another thing troubled Dayton through that winter and spring. That temperament of· his, awakened by an Arab dancer, nursed almost into habit by Claire, and matured and inflamed by Lady Muriel Strange, gave him very little peace. The need, not of any particular woman, but of woman in general, harassed him, joggled his elbow when he drew, and broke his sleep. If he found himself looking forward to marriage as a solution of his difficulties, he felt as if he had smirched a lily. It was as if, having placed his Dorothy upon a pedestal of holiness, he was flinging mud at her.

Though he could not conquer his temperament either by work or by exercise or by wishing, he succeeded at least in holding it in leash. His thoughts at times, however, he could not hold. Sometimes it was as if he, standing aside and begging them by all that was sacred not to, simply revelled in sin and wickedness. In short, he found the strength to keep the letter of faithfulness but not the spirit.

He awakened very early one morning and could

205

His Daughter

not go to sleep again. A deep-throated bell struck
three times. He felt feverish and unhappy. He
tried to think of Dorothy and the sweetness and
trustfulness that would be their life together. Instead he kept thinking of the night when Claire
had not gone home; of the night when Lady Muriel
had said: "Don't be a fool. Kiss me."

Presently he got up, washed his face and hands,
put on his bath-robe, and went out into the hall.
It was not unusual for his mother to be awake
at that hour. If she happened to be awake now
he would pay her a little visit, and they would
talk about Dorothy.

But no light came through his mother's door.
He listened attentively and heard the murmuring
of his mother's voice. Then he knocked very
gently, and a moment later the door was opened
a few inches, and, the heavy portière which had
been drawn across it being displaced, he saw that
there was a light in the room and in that light he
saw the troubled and grieved face of the night
nurse.

"Is my mother awake?" he whispered.

"She's very bad to-night," said the nurse.
"She wouldn't want you to see her, Mr. Dayton."

"She's suffering?"

"She's having one of her attacks. You can't
do anything. Nobody can. Go away, please.

His Daughter

She's given orders. She doesn't want you to see her suffer."

At that moment a voice rose in the room. It was a calm, dispassionate voice that spoke with clear emphasis and was more moving to the lis-teners than screaming.

"This *is* bad!" said the voice. "Heavenly Father, this is *very* bad. This is more than I can bear. This ought to be the last time I am asked to go through such pain. God help me! Christ spare me! Christ, if by any chance you remember how it felt when they drove the nails through your hands and insteps, spare me!"

Then there was silence.

"She is dying!" exclaimed Dayton.

The nurse shook her head.

"No—no—no! Please go away. She'll find that you are here. She'll never forgive me. She doesn't want you to know."

"I'm not a child," said Dayton. "I must know and have my share of this torture." And he pushed past her into the room. But Mrs. Dayton's paroxysm was over just as if Christ had actually recalled the pain of the nails and decided for the moment to spare her. Exhausted almost to the point of death, she had fallen into a deep sleep. Her handsome face looked as if it had been cut out of gray stone.

His Daughter

Dayton's nerves went all to pieces. It was all he could do to restrain his sobs until he got out of the room. He blundered back to his bed, sobbing like a child, and, strangely enough, sleep came to him. It was as if his strength had been utterly exhausted.

It was noon of the next day before his mother sent for him. Neither of them referred to the night; but the mother knew that the son knew, and there was thenceforth to the end a stronger and tenderer bond between them.

To see her son actually settled before she died had become an obsession with Mrs. Dayton. So she took the matter into her own hands and in the end, being a strong-willed and persuasive woman, had her way. In securing Dorothy's co-operation and Dayton's she had no difficulty; and Mrs. Grandison and her husband, finding it impossible to refuse the sick woman's request, gave their half-hearted consent to an early marriage. It was only inwardly, however, that their consent was half-hearted. To Mrs. Dayton, to the young people, to their friends, and to the world at large they showed, not resignation, but what seemed genuine enthusiasm. "As long as it must be," they said to each other, "it is best for every one concerned now, and in the long run, that we appear delighted with the arrangement."

They were very quietly married at Mrs. Dayton's bedside. The bishop of New York presided, and only Dorothy's parents and her brothers were present. Dayton was embarrassed and ill at ease. Everybody was except the bishop, Mrs. Dayton, and Dorothy.

Even her brothers thought that they had never seen so lovely a face. In her eyes was a light that never was on sea or land. Her voice, her beauty, her dignity transformed the sick-room into a chapel. She did not need silk and point-lace to make her look altogether bewitching.

Dayton's heart swelled and yearned with sorrow and faithfulness, for he knew very well that, much as he loved her, he could never love her as she deserved to be loved. It seemed to him almost awful that she should be giving herself to him. The thought that very soon now he must possess her body as already he possessed her soul obtruded and gave him, not pleasure, but pain. Oh, if only he had for her the same gifts of purity and single-heartedness that she had for him! To have been at the moment a man who, though tempted, had remained pure, he would have given, without a moment's hesitation, his right hand.

His Daughter

Had she enough worldly wisdom to know that the average man is not pure? Would she ever ask him questions? No. She had a love and loyalty that would sweep all possible doubts away. But if such questions ever should come up, he knew very well that he would not tell her the truth. He would lie; and she would believe him. He would lie, he told himself, only because it would be kinder to lie.

He had kissed her. They were man and wife. And presently, with no throwing of rice or slippers, they had departed on their honeymoon. It was to be very short. They were going for a few days to a little cottage on Long Island that a friend of Dayton's had loaned him. Their baggage had preceded them.

To Dayton the quiet, well-trained servants that had been loaned with the house had about a thousand eyes apiece. They seemed furtive, spying creatures; the kind of servants who, when doors are suddenly opened in plays, are discovered to have been kneeling at the keyhole. To Dorothy the servants seemed friendly human beings. She was not ashamed of love or any of its manifestations. And with all her heart and soul she looked forward to belonging utterly to her husband. She was without fear or false modesty.

It seemed to Dayton in those first days of his

marriage that a man and his wife might be mentally as far apart as the poles and yet find happiness if their desire was greatly to each other. But mentally he and Dorothy were by no means far apart. They had a hundred tastes in common; indeed, their mental systems had come into such close contact that often one would laughingly snatch the remainder of a phrase from the other's mouth.

Dayton had sometimes thought that Dorothy was of too fine and fastidious a strain to bring to the facts of marriage anything but a dutiful submission. He was entirely mistaken. Her love for him had no reticences. She was neither bold nor shy. She rejoiced openly in the fact that he was a man and that she was a woman.

And so passed nearly a week with its happy chatterings, its delirious and its splendid silences. Then in the night some one knocked on their door, and Dayton, his heart full of fear, rose and went down-stairs and listened at the telephone, and said that he would come as soon as possible. Then there was a frantic midnight dressing, a hasty throwing of a few necessaries into travelling-bags, and a law-breaking motor drive back to the city and to the house from which word had come to them that Mrs. Dayton was dying.

It was a moment which Dayton had lived so

often in anticipation of that his faculties seemed numbed to its actualities. He had pictured and steeled himself to a scene of heart-breaking fare-wells. He had imagined childishly that dying persons remained until the very last moment in full possession of their faculties. It did not seem to him possible that he could face a person who was about to undergo so tremendous an experience. It seemed to him almost as if he ought not to look at his mother.

The disease had eaten down the wall of a deep-seated artery, and at first slowly and now very rapidly she was bleeding to death. Already she had lapsed into complete unconsciousness and was beyond the reach of all heartaches and anxieties.

Dayton and Dorothy had reached the house in time to be with her when she died. But at what precise moment her soul crossed the border line which is drawn between life and death they did not know. Dayton thought that she was still alive when the doctor laid a hand on his shoulder and said a few words in his natural tone of voice (hitherto he had spoken in a hushed voice), and Dayton understood that his mother was dead.

He felt no emotion suitable to the occasion; only a kind of lassitude and a general emptiness.

His Daughter

Yet not to save his life would he have suggested a cup of coffee. He knelt by his mother's bed and kissed her granite-gray forehead, then he realized that Dorothy had slid her arm around him and was drawing him from the room. She made him go down-stairs to the dining-room, where, unknown to her husband, she had ordered coffee to be served. There was a coal fire, all the lights were lighted, and the coffee-urn gleamed at one end of the dark, polished table.

"I'm glad it's over," he said. "Nobody knows how terribly she suffered."

"Shall I pour the coffee?"

Dayton smiled at her a little grimly.

"I don't know what is the matter with me," he said. "I don't feel the way I know I ought to feel. I only feel as if I was very empty and had been up all night. It can't be because I haven't any heart, because one night I heard her when she was suffering and I sobbed and cried like a child."

But some emotion was working in him, for when he lifted his cup of coffee his hand shook so that the contents slopped over into the saucer.

A thousand times during their engagement and their brief honeymoon he had called her his treasure—his comfort. But not until now had she

had the chance to prove that these were not mere
terms of endearment.

Of his bereavement, of her wish that she might
restore his mother to him, she said nothing. She
behaved with perfect naturalness, and even in the
trying conditions of a room harshly lighted at
three o'clock in the morning managed to look
lovely. She made him drink a cup of coffee, and
as soon as she had heard from his own lips that he
couldn't possibly touch a mouthful of food, she
had some eggs boiled and made him eat them.
Then she announced, in the tone of voice of one
accustomed to such experiences, that they would
need all their energies to go through with the work
of the next few days and that it was time to turn
in and get some sleep.

Left to himself, Dayton would have made a
point of suffering as much as possible. But in
Dorothy's hands he was as wet clay. She trun-
dled him off to bed, and there, wrapped in her firm
and tender arms, he shed those tears which it was
natural that he should shed, and slept presently
—all still and peaceful, like a little child.

All through the next day he kept wondering
where, when, and how Dorothy had learned to
do so many things. To arrange for even a simple
modern funeral is only less complicated than mo-

His Daughter

bilizing an army. Where had Dorothy learned the ropes? Who had told her just how many notices there must be in the papers? How did you get a notice into a paper, anyway? How did you know they would print it for you? Where had she learned the red-tapes of churches? Who had told her that Mrs. Dayton wished to be buried in St. Peter's churchyard, Westchester? She even had no trouble in finding out the name of the organist of that church and in communicating to him by telephone the numbers of the hymns which Mrs. Dayton had wished to have sung at her funeral. When and how had Dorothy learned the names of those hymns? She was a miracle —that wife of his. Before breakfast she had interviewed all the servants, given the orders, and taken over the management of the house. And, later in the day, she showed that the death-chamber itself had for her neither strangeness nor difficulties. She was in and out of it as naturally as if it had been a garden, attending to all that needed attention with loving and unflagging efficiency.

Toward afternoon the gray look went out of Mrs. Dayton's face and gave place to a youthful and tender coloring, the grimly set mouth relaxed and seemed to smile. Dorothy had taken posses-

sion of the dead woman's writing-desk. Here she
found time to write brief notes of thanks to those
who had already added to the general complica-
tions by sending flowers and to file for future
answering the despatches and letters that had
already begun to come in.

Late that night Mrs. Dayton was lifted from
her bed to her coffin and carried down to the
drawing-room, where the funeral services were to
be held on the day following.

Dayton shut himself up in his own room while
this was going on. But Dorothy saw the business
through. Her husband, she thought afterward,
when he came to think about it, would be glad.
It was a trying business for Dorothy. Years afterward one phase of it had power to torment her
memory. Mrs. Dayton's right arm had stiffened
at quite an interval from her side. It stuck out
like the wing of a trussed fowl, and it took the
united strength of the undertaker and his assistant
to force it into the coffin.

The door of Dayton's room opened softly.

"Will you come down to the drawing-room and
see if everything's all right?"

He came obediently. They paused by the door
of his mother's room. He swallowed hard. Into
that room he would never go running again with

His Daughter

his little joys and his little troubles—sure of sympathy, sure of comfort, sure of justice.

When they had entered the drawing-room he left Dorothy and walked straight to the coffin and stood for a little while looking at his mother's face. The face was smiling, and so he smiled.

Then, upon a sudden impulse, he took up that section of the coffin cover which goes over the head of the coffin, put it in place, and screwed down the thumbscrews. Then he turned to Dorothy.

"You'll have to arrange the flowers a little differently," he said. "But she looked so happy and smiling. I want to remember her like that. And I don't see any reason why outsiders should come and stare at her. . . . Dorothy, darling, I can't tell you how grateful I am to you for everything, and if—if I'm not good to you always, God torture me!"

VI

AS nearly as the historian can judge, Nature, who never sleeps, had seized joyously upon the very first occasion which the Daytons had offered her to justify their marriage in the eyes of men and gods and each other.

Dayton must have had prophetic qualities, for he loved his child before she was born. That love came to him even with the first suspicion that there was going to be a child. It became almost emotional with the certainty. Already was established that bond, transcending, perhaps, in beauty and unselfishness all other bonds, which sometimes attaches a father to his daughter.

The historian has failed lamentably if he has not made it very clear that Dayton's emotions were easily led. But it would be difficult to produce a man in whom was no faithfulness whatever. And from the moment of her arrival in the world Dayton had for his daughter a veritable passion of understanding and attachment which was never to become stereotyped or stale. He always regretted that he had not had the daring to see her born. He had missed her first cry and

His Daughter

the first half-hour of her existence. That he had failed his wife during the hours when she had most needed him never occurred to him. He had offered to be present. She had said that she would not have him present for anything, and he, average blundering man that he was, had believed her. Not many men subject themselves to the ordeal of seeing a child come into the world. That is a mistake. For when a man asks a girl to marry him he should be able to say: "I love her enough to make up even *that* to her."

She had blue eyes. She yawned in his face calmly and with studied insolence, as a lion yawns. She smiled a wide-open, a gummy, a delectable smile. She gripped his finger. The warmth of her hand, shaped like a clinging starfish, leaped like an electric current to his heart. And this beat like that of an untrained man who has just run swiftly up a steep stair. Still gripping his finger, she slept.

He had been through a great emotional experience. For twenty hours, and for his sake, a woman had been in anguish. From her mouth, the home of a soft and lovely voice, chapped now by chloroform, there came only a hoarse whisper. Dorothy looked so thin and wasted he thought she must be dying. That the nurse laughed at

His Daughter

his fears did not diminish the fact that he had experienced them . . . still gripping his finger, the little daughter slept. Tears gathered in Dayton's eyes, and overflowed and ran down his cheeks.

It was one of those highly concentrated moments when the good that a man has done, the evil, his failures, his success, no longer have a place even in his subconsciousness. There existed for Dayton nothing but the intensity of emotion which had been roused in him by a yawn, a smile, and the grip of a little hand.

If at that moment a spirit had touched him on the shoulder and said: "Your wife is not the only woman who has gone through hell for you, nor is this red and wrinkled thing your only daughter. But you have never seen the other. She too, in the first hour of her life, yawned and smiled, and she would have gripped too, if you had been there to hold out your finger to her. But there were only poor Claire D'Avril and the slovenly old midwife—" It is doubtful if Dayton would have heard.

A judgment of Dayton should not be without leniency. If he had known that Claire D'Avril was to have a baby he would not have deserted her. He was not the kind of man who makes an

His Daughter

open issue with fate. It is quite likely that, led by emotion and real tenderness, and driven by remorse, he might have married her. We do know that, baby or no baby, he had every intention of keeping her supplied with money and even, for a time, with love. Some men would have kept on writing letters longer than Dayton did; for constancy varies in duration, not intensity; but no man, if never an answer came to any of the letters, would have kept on writing them forever. Because he yielded easily to temptation is no proof that Dayton did not know the difference between right and wrong. He knew it perfectly well, and he honestly felt that he had given Claire D'Avril a square deal. He honestly thought that she must have received some of his letters and, for reasons easily guessed, was ashamed to answer them. A girl of her temperament and domestic instincts could not exist for very long without love. Sometimes, with an odd feeling of jealousy, he wondered what the new lover was like.

But Marie Claire's temperament and domestic instincts had not yet thrown her into the arms of another lover.

There were no loving hearts to give Claire D'Avril support and courage as her time drew near. There was no specialist to come to her at sixty miles an hour in case anything went wrong. With the exception of her own brave, aching heart, she had nothing that Dorothy had—not even money. She would have, when she had paid the greedy old midwife, a dark and narrow room with no rugs upon its stone floor, a hard little bed, a stiff little chair, a jug of water if she chose to fetch it, and her baby.

But one day, sick and frightened, as she sat looking out of her own window at the only pretty thing that was hers to look at—the blue sky— there was a sharp knocking on the door, and a moment later Arnold Charnowski was filling the room with his vivid and spectacular personality.

"You have not come to me lately," he said, "to see if there was any letter. So I became anxious and came to you."

"How did you find out where I lived?"

"As a rule," said Charnowski, with the most engaging frankness, "I prefer mysteries to facts; but this is a very simple case. I paid a small boy to follow you. Pardon me, but you have come to the end of your money?"

"I shall have nothing to go on with," said Claire, "but I shall find work."

"After some weeks—yes. But in the meantime?"

His Daughter

She did not answer.

"Don't be so distant with me. I wished to be your lover; you did not wish that. Very well, it is over. Now I wish to be your friend. Don't you want my friendship either? . . . You silly child, I ask nothing of you, except the privilege to be of service. God has wished to deceive if he has not written in my face that I have a heart."

"I would like to trust you," said Claire, in a small voice, "but——"

"You are lonely and in trouble, yet it gives you no pleasure to see me. You would rather starve than take the help I offer. It's pathetic. Do you think your baby will feel the same way? How do you know what your baby is going to think about starving—you who do not even know whether that baby is to be a boy or a girl? You are absurd."

Claire D'Avril turned her head and seemed to be looking at the blue sky; but she could not see it, because her eyes had filled with tears.

"I refuse," said Charnowski gently, "to puff out my chest and blow about the kind of man I am. There is no use telling you that I am honest and mean to do right. If you do not feel these things instinctively, nothing that I can say is going to change you. It is true that I like pretty women; but I am no fool. I know perfectly well when a woman is not for me. I have learned to like you and respect you for yourself. That has nothing to do with your good looks. I wish to be your friend and to help you. But you do not trust me. I read you like a book. You believe that I have a fixed end in view; that offers of disinterested friendship and of help are only a cloak to my inherent baseness. You are even planning to change your habitation, so that the next time I shall not be able to find you. You think that I am a sort of spider who is trying to catch you in a net of hypocrisy. . . . My dear child, I understand perfectly. It is natural that you should feel toward me as you do; and yet it is a great pity. Still, if you will not let me act for you directly, I must do what I can indirectly. I shall speak to your uncle."

Claire D'Avril was on her feet in an instant.

"You mustn't do that. Already he has done more for me than he has any right to do. I have gone out of their lives. They think I have gone away somewhere with my friend They do not know that I am in want—deserted. . . . If you told them, I could find it in my heart to kill you!"

Charnowski nodded gravely, as if he understood perfectly.

His Daughter

"If there were degrees of impossibility," he said, "the most impossible thing would be to go back to that home from which we have set forth so gayly and so confidently and to confess that we have failed utterly. . . ." He struck his right fist energetically into the palm of his left hand and in a vibrant voice exclaimed: "Catch me going home and confessing that the world has yet to hear me."

"You too?" asked Claire. "Have you failed?"

"Not yet!" said Charnowski, and his voice was like the snapping of a coach-whip. He paced the room for half a minute, by turns frowning and smiling. Then he broke into a good-natured laugh.

"You'd rather take help from me than from your uncle. Is that a fact?"

"Yes," said Claire.

"We have, then, one bond in common. I would rather touch Satan for a loan than my own father, whom I love and revere, and who would lend gladly, because he still believes in me. Let's have no more nonsense, young lady. I will see you through your trial, and then, if you wish no more of my friendship—" he snapped his strong fingers and said "Phtt!"

Every day or so Charnowski came to see her;

sometimes he stayed a long time; sometimes he only looked in for a moment. He was kind and practical, but reserved. She began to believe in his friendship. And, though she had as yet taken no money from him, she acquired toward him feelings of obligation and gratitude. And she talked very frankly with him about her future.

Deep in Claire D'Avril's heart was the notion that Dayton would come back to her some day, and that when he discovered that there was a child he might wish to marry her. There would be a time of hardship and temptation, but in the end there would be plenty and happiness. In this belief Charnowski encouraged her. He was a subtle man.

One day he could not conceal that he was elated over something.

"We are in luck," he said. "I have found an excellent position for you. That good old Larrousse who conducts the Tête D'Or, where I take most of my meals, has dismissed his *dame du comptoir*. I have spoken to him very strongly on your behalf. He is going to give you a trial. In the meanwhile his daughter has consented to keep the books. The pay is good, the hours are not long. You accept. It is understood."

"But I must have work that I can do here."

His Daughter

Charnowski shook his head. "You will live at the Tête D'Or," he said. "You will have time not only to make the change for the customers, and to keep the old man's books, but to look after your baby as well. All that will arrange itself beautifully. It is one of the reasons why I appear so conceited and pleased with myself. But you shall not work until you are able. A few weeks' rest; that will not cost you much. You will accept that rest as a loan from me. Out of your wages you shall pay me back. Now be nice! Say to yourself: 'This poor Charnowski is really trying to be my friend,' and accept!"

"How kind you are!" exclaimed Claire.

"Larrousse is a good old soul," said Charnowski. "You know his place, of course. Middle-class, if you like, but quiet and respectable. It is not frequented by the type of men who might annoy you."

Charnowski called again the next day; but Claire D'Avril had company. For some hours she had been a mother. But it was more as if she had gone out into the streets, seen a baby that she fancied, and brought it home with her. A little pale, a little tremulous, she was up and dressed. And already she had been on an errand.

"It is classic! It is Roman!" exclaimed Charnowski. And his eyes, full of wonder, roved from Claire D'Avril to the tiny, emotionless figure, closely swaddled, that lay on one of the pillows at the head of the bed.

Claire D'Avril couldn't help boasting a little.

"In all Madame Aimée's experience," she said, "it has never happened so easily before. What would you? I am not without courage. I did everything she told me to, and never cried out at all. But perhaps you think it was pleasant!"

"May I look?"

Charnowski stepped swiftly to the bed, and Claire D'Avril drew aside the swaddling-clothes so that he could see the baby's face.

"But," he exclaimed, "that is not a wrinkled-up monkey; it is a human being. It has hair and dimples. That is not an ordinary baby at all. That is a little cabbage, a treasure."

After that speech Claire D'Avril had no longer any mistrust of Arnold Charnowski. Her heart warmed to him.

"But tell me," he said. "It's a son?"

"Oh, no," she exclaimed indignantly.

"Good," said Charnowski, "I prefer daughters. They do not come home smelling of absinthe and cigarettes."

They both laughed. Presently, with gentle gravity, he said:

His Daughter

"And my friendship? You have decided to accept that?"

"Yes," said Claire D'Avril, "I have misjudged you. I am sorry."

"It is nothing," he said.

"And in a very few days," she said, "I can go to the Tête D'Or. And then I can begin paying you back."

Out of her first week's wages she had expected to make a payment to Charnowski; but the destitute condition in which the baby had come into the world had tempted her into divers extravagances. Charnowski only laughed. He said he did not care if she never paid him. But two months later she owed neither Charnowski nor any other man a penny. If this was a discomfiture to Charnowski he swallowed it with good grace.

"Frankly," he told her, "I am glad. It is difficult to believe in the disinterestedness of those to whom we owe money. But are you happy here?"

"I am secure," said Claire. "Père Larrousse is a good man. My baby has never had a day's illness. The *habitués* of the place are a decent lot. But happiness? That is a strong word. For more often I feel like crying than laughing."

"I admire your courage," said Charnowski.

"It is your finest quality. But I had hoped that with the baby to think about you would soon forget. Tell me, does the wound still smart as cruelly as it did at first?"

"Why, yes," said Claire, "but I have not so much time to think of what I have lost."

"You should try to forget."

"I don't want to forget. Why should I pretend that I have not lived and been happy? It would be a folly and a pose. And besides, I think he will come back. When he knows about the little girl he will come back."

"When he knows, perhaps—yes! But these Americans! How do they ever find out anything? Do you know that if our beautiful country were picked up and dropped on the United States it would resemble only a very small stamp on a very large envelope? And if the years pass, and he does not come back? How will you establish yourself? I speak not for the purpose of hurting your feelings but out of friendship. It is your worst fault that you do not try to look far into the future. You do not always expect to be a *dame du comptoir*, I suppose?"

Claire D'Avril shook her head. "I dream," she said, smiling, "that I shall save enough money to establish myself in a little business. In the meanwhile—thanks to you—I have a position which satisfies me."

Charnowski gathered up the change which she had made for him, and slipped it into his trouser pocket.

"You do not come any more to inquire if there is a letter?"

"I do not expect that one will come now," she said simply.

"But the studio, where you were so happy; nothing is changed. Aren't you ever going to pay me a little visit and drink a cup of tea? I am a little hurt that you haven't come of your own accord. It's as if you did not feel sure of me. Will you come some day and bring the baby? Then I will know that we are really to be friends."

"I will come to-morrow," said Claire. "Between three and five, when I am not needed here."

"I hope you will come at three and stay till five," said Charnowski gallantly.

But it was a little past four when she stepped once more into the familiar room. Her heart was beating quickly. It was not an easy moment for her.

But Charnowski, by behaving as if she were in

the habit of coming, made it as easy as he could. He behaved with perfect naturalness.

Over the statue which Dayton had made of Claire a sheet was draped. And for this piece of consideration she was grateful. But neither of them made any reference to the statue. Presently Claire D'Avril began to scold Charnowski.

"You have been idle," she said. "You made me believe that you were working your hands off, and yet I don't see as much as a sketch. Where is the famous picture for the Salon?"

Charnowski indicated the fireplace.

"It made a fine blaze," he said. "Indeed, I have burned everything. But to-morrow I have a new model coming, and I shall begin again from the beginning." He pointed to a fresh canvas in place on the big easel.

"I have had rotten luck with models," he went on. "Only those, it seems, who are ugly and badly made go into the business. But I am trying a new one to-morrow. Her face is not bad. As for the rest, we shall see what we shall see." He shrugged his shoulders and turned to the piano.

"Fortunately," he said, "I play a little. And when I am utterly discouraged I play and I forget."

And, as if one of those moments of depression

His Daughter

was upon him, he stepped brusquely to the piano, swept the sheets of music with which it was heaped to the floor, flung open the top, seated himself, and struck a chord that was like a clap of thunder. For a quarter of an hour it was as if a storm were raging in the studio.

Even Claire D'Avril, who did not know one note from another, was affected by the power and the virtuosity of Charnowski's playing. There were moments when it seemed as if he had twenty strong hands instead of only two. He took her breath away. But it was not the beauty of the music which affected her; it was the volume and the speed. She would have been similarly affected by seeing a man jump from the top of a high building.

Charnowski had played to deaf ears and he knew it. But, as he turned from the piano, Claire's baby, who had been struggling and wriggling, suddenly stretched forth both its tiny hands and crowed with delight.

Almost roughly Charnowski took the baby from Claire and carried her to the window. She crowed again. And he looked into her mouth. Then he looked at her ears. They were thin and delicate and very flat to her head. He carried her to the piano, and holding her with his

233

His Daughter

left arm, played a charming little accompaniment with his right hand, and sang very softly and sweetly to her. Claire could not understand the words.

While he was singing the baby kept as still as a mouse. But when he had finished she wriggled strongly, and crowed at the top of her lungs. Again he played and sang, and again the baby listened, and again, when he had finished, did her best to applaud.

"It is a miracle," said Charnowski simply; "she is one in ten million. I wish to God she was mine. I wonder if it has ever happened in the world before? They tell extraordinary tales of Mozart and of our own Chopin; but this cabbage three times has crowed on the same key in which I was playing!"

As if she had been a precious vase of paper-thin porcelain he returned the baby to her mother's arms.

"The father," he said, "must have had more music in him than I have gathered from his exercise-books. Be very careful of her, Claire D'Avril. It may be that some day she will be famous from one end of Europe to the other. I myself, when she is a little older, will give her lessons. See, she wants to come to me."

His Daughter

"And that is also a miracle," Claire laughed, "because it is her dinner-time."

Claire colored a little.

"Do you mind?" she said.

"Of course not. I will make some toast for tea."

He went into the little kitchen and closed the door behind him.

The Countess de Ségour had never heard of Arnold Charnowski; but she liked Poles as a rule and sent word that she would receive him.

Neither the countess's luxurious surroundings nor the fact that his own clothes were a little shabby troubled Charnowski. He was quite at his ease. He thanked her for receiving him, and gave his excuse for having ventured to call upon her.

"I have rented the studio which was formerly your brother's," he said. "He seems to have left behind him certain belongings of a purely personal nature and, while these things are not actually in my way, I feel a certain responsibility about them. Briefly, madam, I should like his address."

"I will give you that very willingly," said the countess, and she wrote it out upon a slip of paper. "You knew my brother?"

His Daughter

"I have not that pleasure. And yet I feel as if I know him. He modelled a little, drew a little, painted a little, played a little, composed a little, and left Paris suddenly, owing no man money. And so I have pictured to myself an honest, hardworking young man who will perhaps make a name for himself. You have good reports of him, I hope."

"Excellent," said the countess.

"We may look for his return one of these days?"

"I think he will settle in America. He has married a charming girl, and I suppose for the rest of his life will think more about his income than his art."

"Married?" said Charnowski, and there came into his eyes a sudden flash of elation. This did not escape Dayton's sister.

"She was little more than a child," she said, "but my mother, who was dying, wished it, and the marriage was made. It is turning out very happily."

"I am glad to hear that," said Charnowski. "But he will find that marriage is not good for art."

"You believe that?"

"Yes, madam."

"Why?"

236

His Daughter

"Marriage," he said, "is a commercialism of youth, ardor, and ambitions. The difference between a work of art and a pot-boiler may be no more than the price of a couple of seats in the gallery or a new blouse."

"You are an artist, of course?"

"*I* think so," said Charnowski, "but I have never been heard of."

"You paint?"

"For fun only. Unless I am greatly mistaken I am a musician. You like music?"

"I even studied for years," said the countess, "but there was something lacking."

"Always," said Charnowski, "there is something lacking. The painter cannot draw; the composer cannot play; the well-beloved loves another; there is a worm in the peach. One is at peace reading the latest scandal in yellow covers, and one is interrupted by an importunate *rôle*."

He rose, and held out his hand.

"I thank you," he said, "for your graciousness to me."

"It is so easy," said the countess, "to be gracious to charming people."

When he had gone she wished that she had asked him to call again. She was always drawn to people who were not affected by their surround-

237

ings. And in addition she wanted to know why
Charnowski had received the news of her brother's
marriage with evidences of pleasure.

Charnowski carried away from the interview a
light heart. He was now great friends with Claire
D'Avril, and he believed that, upon the definite
news of Dayton's faithlessness, this friendship
might soon ripen into something else. But he
put off telling her for several days. He was afraid
that the elation which he felt might show in his
face and spoil everything. He actually rehearsed
what he should say to her, watching his expression
in the looking-glass over the bureau.

One day he dropped into the Tête D'Or between
hours, and hurried at once to her tall desk in the
corner.

"My dear friend," he said, "I have bad news
for you. If I haven't proved to you that I have
your interest at heart, it isn't for want of trying.
When I learned that Frederick Dayton had a sister living in Paris, I called upon her. I made the
excuse that he had left behind him certain personal
belongings, for which I did not care to be responsible. I asked boldly for his address. She wrote
it for me on a piece of paper. Here it is, if you
wish to write to him."

His Daughter

Claire D'Avril was trembling all over.

"My poor child," said Charnowski, "you will need all your courage. Fate has been unkind to you. Frederick Dayton was called suddenly back to America by the illness of his mother. Literally on her death-bed she forced him to contract a marriage with the young lady she had picked out for him."

Claire D'Avril's eyes filled with tears and she said gently:

"It was right for him to do what his mother wished."

"Yes," said Charnowski, "it would not be fair to say that he has acted badly. But now that you have his exact address you will, I hope, be businesslike. You should tell him about the little daughter and hope that he will do the right thing."

But Claire D'Avril shook her head, and after one despairing look at the piece of paper with Dayton's address she tore it into small pieces.

"Perhaps life is hard for him too," she said.

From this time Charnowski noted a new restlessness in Claire D'Avril. She seemed no longer content to cast up accounts for old Larrousse and to make change for his customers.

239

His Daughter

"It will get me nowhere," she said. "The little daughter has no one to look to but me. Somehow I must earn more money, so that she will never want for anything."

"But you are saving money."

"Even if I saved, as I am saving now, for ten years, I should have very little. Life is hard for a woman."

"It will be no easier in ten years," said Charnowski, "unless in the meantime you strike it rich."

He sighed wearily, and added:

"Life is hard for men too. Look at me. I have talent, and yet if it were not for the rent of a little house in Warsaw I should starve. I have inexhaustible energy and I cannot make a living. My heart is tender, but I do not inspire affection."

He tossed his head and laughed.

A day or two later Claire wheeled her baby to the studio on Charnowski's invitation. The place smelt of burnt paint and the fireplace contained a wreck of canvas and framework three parts consumed.

"Your new picture?" asked Claire, full of pity and sympathy.

"My model turned out a fool," he said. "It was a pleasure to burn even the image I had made

His Daughter

of her. I shall not waste any more money on experiments. I am good for nothing except to amuse children." He held out his hands for the baby and she crowed with delight. He carried her to the piano and played for her and sang to her.

On this afternoon, while Claire nursed her baby, Charnowski did not go out of the room; but he turned his back frankly and made a great show of bringing order among the massed and messed sheets of music under which the piano was half-buried. But the mere knowledge that in the same room with him the woman he desired sat with her breast bare drove the blood into his face and made his hands tremble.

If he had looked directly at her, Claire would not have minded. For it was the custom of her class to nurse its babies in public.

"Well, has she finished?"

"And getting ready for her nap."

"Let me hold her."

The baby went to sleep in Charnowski's arms; but for some time he continued to pace the studio slowly, his eyes intent upon the child's face. After a time he made a nest for her among the sofa-cushions and laid her in it.

"Now it's our turn," he said, and he pulled his

241

His Daughter

tea-table into the middle of the room and lighted the spirit-lamp.

"It is nice here," said Claire D'Avril. "At first it hurt me terribly to come; but I am glad now that I have broken the ice."

"It is fine for me," said Charnowski. "I have few friends. I look forward to your visits and back upon them. Also I love the little daughter. But I think you should give her a name. We could have a christening—just ourselves and the priest and two or three friends. I shall be godfather. What are you going to name her? Remember that she is going to be a famous musician."

"Then she mustn't have my name," said Claire. "You yourself have said that I don't know the difference between do and fa."

"And that is true," Charnowski laughed boyishly; "you don't. You have no music in you at all. It is quite a distinction. It is almost as distinguished and rare as to be a musician of the very first water."

"It is fortunate that you have pretty ears."

"Have I?"

"Everything about you is pretty, and you know it."

He turned abruptly, walked to the window, and

looked out. After a moment he returned, with a look of resolution.

"Do you want to do me a favor, Claire?"

"Of course."

"You won't misunderstand me? If it's a favor that you can't grant, just say no and forget that it was asked. Will you pose for me?"

She did not answer at once.

"I've tried a dozen models," he went on in a matter-of-fact tone. "And you know the results. It amounts to this: I have wasted months of time and oceans of energy, and have nothing to show. It is vital that I paint a successful picture. With you for a model I should not fail. It is only one friend asking help of another."

Not once but many times, out of gratitude for the way in which he had stood by her, Claire had said to Charnowski: "If there is ever any way in which I can help you, you will tell me."

Now he had told her in what way she could help him; and, because it was a way the idea of which was disagreeable to her, it looked as if professions of friendship and of service were going to fail at the first test. Her face and neck turned a dull red.

Charnowski shrugged his shoulders.

His Daughter

"We will say no more about it," he said a little stiffly. "But it is hard for an artist to see things from the point of view of a person who is not an artist: to me a beautiful body is merely a thing of beauty; to you it is a brazen piece of immodesty."

For the second time he shrugged his shoulders, but ever so slightly.

"It isn't that I don't want to help you," said Claire; "you know that. But—why, it's almost as if you asked me for something that I haven't got."

"You wouldn't mind as much as you think," said Charnowski. "There would be the first little shock, like getting into cold water—but we will say no more about it."

Claire nodded toward the statue of herself, swathed in the dusty sheet.

"Couldn't you paint from that?" she asked.

"Is your body the color of dry clay?" he asked, "or is it some other color? But I understand your point of view. I myself am as modest as the next man. I should not be capable of taking off my clothes and going for a stroll in the Luxembourg Gardens. Even if a friend asked me to pose for him as an act of friendship, the idea would embarrass me. But surely if it was a question of his career, or if he thought it was, I should swallow my embarrassment—and pose."

No more was said about the matter at that time. Charnowski even seemed to have dismissed it entirely from his mind. But Claire thought of it often, and it troubled her. For she felt that through her squeamishness she was failing a tried friend in friendship.

Claire had a friend who was a model. One day she met her in the street, and after greetings——

"Tell me," said Claire, "you who pose for artists, was it very terrible the first time?"

Puriette La Soule laughed.

"I was sixteen," she said. "My mother went with me. I was to pose for Papa Gouriot, who was a million years old. But I was frightened to death, and while I screamed and kicked they undressed me by force. Even then I would not pose. Papa Gouriot cleared everything out of the studio behind which I could hide or with which I could cover myself. Then he sat down before his canvas with an air of patience and waited. My mother was for action, but after a time he made her go into an adjoining room and locked the door. He had done the same by the street door, and he had both the keys in his pocket. As for me, I

245

had tried to blot myself out in the darkest corner of the room. Then he began to talk very gently:

"'The good Lord made you, my poor little Puriette,' he said, 'with infinite pains.'

"And then he told me a million things about my bones and lungs and my heart and my joints that I had never dreamed before.

"'And all this,' he said, 'the Lord God covered with the most wonderful and beautiful of all fabrics. But you, sitting in judgment on the Lord's work, have said: "Only my face and hands are fit to be seen. There is something shameful about the rest of me, something indecent." Is it not so?' But I only glared at him.

"'It is of course true,' he said, 'that your back has a few blemishes——'

"I twisted my head and tried to see my back; but he chuckled, and I knew that he had been dangling a bait and that I had jumped for it. I couldn't help laughing.

"'Stand over in that ray of sunlight,' he said, 'and look at me over your shoulder.'

"I did not move or answer.

"'Very well, then,' he said, 'stay as you are.' And he began to draw.

"Then of course I moved, and I said: 'I hate you; you are an old beast. I want to go away.'

His Daughter

And I began to howl. When I had finished howling he let my mother out of the room in which she was locked, and they went round the corner to have lunch, leaving me naked and hungry and locked in.

"'I will throw myself out of the window,' I shouted after them, but I did no such thing. The studio was up three flights. They did not come back till late—late. It was no longer nice and warm. And I was weak with rage and hunger. I was like a little wild animal that had been brought into the woods, and I was beginning to wish that I was tame.

"Papa Gouriot went at once to his easel.

"'Stand over there,' he said, 'and look at me over your shoulder.'

"To my own surprise, but very sullenly, I did as he told me. And as I stood my eyes filled with tears and I emitted a frightful sneeze.

"Papa Gouriot put back his head and roared with laughter. Then he bustled about and made my mother get my clothes, and he himself pretended to be a *femme de chambre* and was so funny that I had to laugh. But adroit! My dear, what he didn't know about a girl's clothes wasn't worth knowing. He painted me for the Salon; I got so that I didn't mind him any more than I minded myself. And now? Well, the other day I started for the street just as I was! It's gotten so that I have to think hard to remember whether I am dressed or undressed. One thinks only of the fatigue now—keeping in one position for such long times. But what is all this to you? Are you thinking of turning model?"

"I think of it sometimes; but not because of the money. There is a good friend who wishes very much for me to pose for him, and I would like to out of friendship—only I am ashamed and embarrassed."

Puriette La Soule laughed.

"There is nothing to be ashamed of," she said. "And there is nothing to be embarrassed about. Who is he?"

"Arnold Charnowski. Have you ever posed for him?"

"Never."

"We are something alike. Maybe you would do as well. I will speak to him about you."

"That isn't necessary. Give me his address."

Two or three days later Charnowski thanked Claire for sending Puriette to him.

"She hasn't the legs I want," he said, "but her head and shoulders are charming; and better, she is a real character—she makes me laugh."

His Daughter

"It is ridiculous to suppose," said Claire, "that in all Paris no one has the right figure for you except me."

She laughed loudly and nervously and grew red in the face.

"You'll do it?" Charnowski almost snapped the question at her, so great was his eagerness.

"If I don't, you will say that I have spoiled your career."

"When?" he asked.

"The sooner the better. I don't want to have to think about it."

"You are free between nine and eleven. You will come, then, to-morrow? Oh, what a load you have taken off my heart! You are a true friend. You will be glad. But how shall I thank you?"

The next morning, at a few minutes past nine o'clock, Claire arrived at Charnowski's studio. She laughed a good deal with unnatural loudness, and made a pretense of swagger and bluster. She was suffering badly from a sort of stage fright.

She disrobed behind the screen; when she was ready she burst into tears.

VII

THERE passed a period of years during which automobiles became things of beauty and perfection; during which man caused a machine, heavier than the air which it displaced, to rise from the ground and fly; a period during which Frederick Dayton achieved notable success in several of his chosen lines.

Of his occasional escapades it seemed that the whole world knew, but that Dorothy Dayton did not. She presided over their house in town and their house in the country, and over their family goings and comings, with a serenity and affection that seemed to give his reputation the lie. Dorothy had married for life—for happiness or unhappiness. She soon learned that her husband did not love her as a husband should. She soon learned that other women came into his life and went out. And she had hours and whole nights even when she wished she were dead. But she was game to the core. And she would not for the world have let her father and mother know that she was unhappy. She loved her husband long after the respect which she had had for him

was dead in her heart. It was curious, that—
she loved him, she admired him, she forgave him,
she took him back, she did not blame other
women for loving him (she wondered how anybody could help loving him), she rejoiced in his
accomplishments, his successes, his growing celeb-
rity, she thought that the love which he had for
their daughter was the most beautiful love that
she had ever seen—but she did not respect him.

She had given everything that she had to give
—and—well, she clung to the idea that during
the first year of her married life she had received
as much as she gave. She would think:

"I can't say that I haven't had absolute bliss
in my life. I have had. And of course it couldn't
last forever. It never does. It only lasted a
little while; but I've had it, and that's all anybody has a right to expect. And, whatever happens now, I'll remember, I'll remember *hard*, and
then I won't whine."

She had Dayton's respect, gratitude, and admiration. He thought her the most beautiful
woman in the world. He took a tremendous and
creative interest in her costumes; he did some
charming busts of her; and he reproached himself
bitterly at times for ever having loved any one
else. His first act of unfaith tormented him for

His Daughter

a long time. He had tried hard to be a model husband and, as he himself expressed it, "to keep his eyes in the boat." But his temperament was too much for him. More and more remorse lost its power to bite. Romance played less and less often the leading part in his intrigues; more and more models and chorus girls became the important part of his life. With one exception.

There was in Dayton's nature one streak as pure as crystal and as strong as steel. He loved his daughter with a strength and beauty which transcended his own understanding. This love was almost her twin. Its birth coincided with her own; and long before she could speak a word she had showed with all her energy that she returned it in kind. She loved everybody who was connected with her—her mother, her nurse, her grandparents—but that was a mere bountiful overflow from that great reservoir of adoration which she had for her father.

"Oh," Dorothy used often to think, "if he could only have loved me as truly as that!" And it was a very wistful smile she wore sometimes when she heard them romping together or saw them "vanishing into the landscape" upon some exciting adventure.

His Daughter

She was a beautiful child, very strong and straight. She had a fine round head, bright brown hair with a little wave in it. Her eyes were blue and steadfast. She was afraid of nothing. She had a strong will, tempered by good nature and generosity. Among her parents' friends she very early won a reputation for character and ability. What she said she would do she did. Her given word was as good as a bond. She never lied.

Dayton admired her tremendously—her looks, her build, her character. He played boys' games with her by the hour. With a baseball she was better than the average boy of her own age. She could throw a fly nicely; she could shoot nicely with a twenty-two. She could be trusted to drive any of her father's cars. When he came out from town it was always she who met him at the station; but at such times he knew better than to take any liberties with her. She was then a chauffeur. She touched her hat, she opened the door; she put the rug over his knee; and then she drove away with him, proud as Punch.

She was so full of out-of-doors that they had hard work teaching her to read and write. She tried, but the things of out-of-doors kept getting between the thinking parts of her brain and pre-

vented them from getting together. But her
. mother said:

"When father's away you can write letters to
him and tell him about everything here, and he
will write back and tell you about everything
there; and perhaps if you ask him to bring you
something sensible he will do it when he comes
home."

After that the scattered little brain pulled itself
together very quickly, and she learned to read
and write in no time at all.

Sometimes when he was away Dayton had
frights about the child. They were entirely of
his own imagining. But they filled him with excellent excuses for breaking any kind of an engagement and getting home as quickly as possible.

She had talent. She was musical, and she
learned very early to love the smell of clay wet for
the moulding, of oil, paint, turpentine, and such
like. From the first she was able to punch, knead,
and paddle a lump of clay till it looked like something. And Dayton did not for one moment
doubt that she was the most beautiful, talented,
wise, and virtuous child that had ever been born
into the world.

The thought that in the dim future—and not
such a dim future at that—she could love some

His Daughter

man (now probably a total stranger to her) more
than her own father, and go away to live in his
house, and be treated very likely just as her
mother had been, gave him moments of real
anguish.

He could see no happiness in a life where he
had ceased to be her chief concern and interest.
He had the fear, too, that as she grew older she
would in the very nature of things turn more and
more to her mother. He was afraid that some
day she would find out that he had not been good
to her mother, and that the knowledge, little by
little, since for his conduct there was no very good
excuse that could be offered, would embitter her
against him. She wouldn't be rich exactly; but
she would be very well off. There are men in
this world who are capable of securing a girl's
affections and marrying her for her money. He
cursed such men root and branch. Meanwhile,
if only it weren't for soiling memories and fore-
bodings about the future, how happy he was!
How much sheer delight there was in having such
a daughter!

Long before she was old enough to understand
such things he believed that he would be a sedate
and steady man whose conduct should no longer
give grounds for reproach. In cool moments he

did not mince terms, but called himself a beast, a satyr; but nothing that he could call himself helped for very often or very long. One day a young man, a total stranger to Dayton, pushed open the door of his studio and marched in. Dayton looked up with a kind of amazed inquiry in his face.

"Is your name Dayton?"

"Yes. What can I do for you?"

"Frederick Dayton?"

"Yes."

"I wanted to be sure."

The young man pulled a small automatic pistol from his pocket and shot Dayton in the stomach; then turned upon his heel and marched out.

Dayton, who had fallen heavily and then fainted, came to in a few moments and struggled to the telephone. Even while he was giving his doctor's number he was puzzling his brain to remember who that young man could be. To his best belief and knowledge he had never set eyes on him before. Yet not for one moment did he have to search for a possible cause for the shooting. There was more than one man in New York who had a good excuse for shooting him—he was lying on the floor again, just under the telephone —he could not remember whether the doctor had

His Daughter

answered his call or not. . . . It didn't matter.
. . . He guessed he was a goner, doctor or no
doctor. . . . Suddenly he broke into a sweat of
anguish. And once more, with the nerve and
will of a better and stronger man, he dragged himself to his feet, caught up the receiver, and gave
the number of his country house.

"That you, Spagget? I wish to speak to Miss
Ellen—" He waited, swaying and dizzy—he
heard her voice.

"That you, puss? It's father. I can't get
home to-night. I may have to go away for a few
days. Is it cool down there? That's good. It's
been hot as blazes in town. . . . Is mother
handy? I'd like to speak to her. All right, my
darling. . . . So-long!"

He swayed and swayed, the sweat pouring off
him. But he had had his wish. If he was going
to die he had at least managed to hear once more
the sound of her dear voice. Then it was Dorothy speaking. His own voice was now a ghastly
shadow of itself.

"I've been badly hurt," he said, "but don't let
Ellen know. I am at the studio. You had better telephone my doctor and see if he is coming
or not. I tried to tell him, and I don't know
whether I suc—cee—ded or not. . . . I'm sorry

His Daughter

I've been such a rotten bad husband to you.
. . . Don't let Ellen know what I'm really like
—ev—er. *Please* don't, Dorothy——"

He could do no more. He rasped down the
wall, into a position half-standing and half-
crouching, and then fell over on his side.

But Frederick Dayton was not destined to die
of that wound. They got him to a hospital, op-
erated at once, and managed to save him. There
were many rumors, but the story that he had
been suddenly seized with acute appendicitis was
generally believed. And very few persons—and
they were very wise—connected the affair in
any way with the suicide of Frank Tilman, the
rising young comedian. It had taken place within
the hour following Dayton's seizure, and in a
small park just around the corner from Dayton's
studio.

During his convalescence Dayton came across
some reference to Tilman's suicide. "So *that's*
who it was," he thought. The woman who had
caused the bullet to fly had not made a strong
impression on Dayton. Still, she might feel it
her duty to graft on him. He was tired of New
York. Winter was coming on. He went to sleep
thinking of Paris. A little of Paris would be
good for them all—especially Ellen. Now was

His Daughter

the time to make her French golden. He himself would be refreshed by a thousand fresh art impulses. Furthermore, he would be good now. He had had his lesson. Though it killed him he would go no more a-roaming by the light of the moon. What fun he and Ellen could have in Paris! It would bring them closer to each other than ever. She was beginning to enjoy "all those children" down in the country too much. He was frankly jealous of all those children.

"There are too many people in New York," he thought, "who might start something. In Paris——"

He began to think about Claire D'Avril. He had a real tenderness for her. They had been each other's first. They had ventured hand in hand, two timid children, into the dark. "But, oh, my word," he thought, "how much water has rolled under the bridge since then! Fourteen years —more than fourteen years—and only think, I wanted to marry her! And if I had there never would have been any Ellen—no Ellen in all the world!" He pondered that. It was impossible to picture such a world! By no stretch of the imagination could he imagine such a world worth living in. In the morning he talked matters over with his wife—very frankly. A week later they sailed for Bordeaux.

The shock of his recent experience had greatly sobered Dayton. He was very quiet, very gentle, very tender with his wife and daughter. The smoking-room had no charms for him. He made Dorothy realize that she was absolutely necessary to his well-being. And in a hundred ways he tried to make up to her for the past.

She was happier than she had been for many years. She had not wished to go to Paris, but she was very glad that she had given in. The change was doing them all good.

And Paris was so wonderful. She had forgotten how wonderful. It is the city where nothing ever changes. Knights in armor have yielded to the landau, the landau to the motor-car. But Paris does not change. Always for her friends she has the same sweet and cheerful face filled with understanding and good humor.

"I am very happy," thought Dayton. "I have the best wife in the world, and the dearest daughter, and Paris."

The first month of their stay was devoted to sightseeing, to theatre and restaurant life. Then, having rented a pleasant and spacious apartment,

His Daughter

they all, as Dayton expressed it, "went to school."

A governess was found for Ellen, and twice a week—for the child had developed a surprising talent—she had a piano lesson from the famous Charnowski. He was very particular about pupils, and it was only through the influence of the Countess de Séjour that he consented to teach Ellen.

To Dayton the impulse to work had returned, and when he learned that his old studio was untenanted he secured the key from the baleful Madame Sidon and ran lightly up the stairs to have a look at the place.

Madame Sidon had then fled at the sight of him. In her guilty soul she imagined that he had come to ask about his letters to Claire D'Avril. But this was not in his mind. Madame Sidon had always shown the handsome American her best sides. He remembered her with pleasure.

"Monsieur Sidon?"

He was dead. Dayton expressed his sorrow. He had liked the old man.

"Since my time," he said, "I suppose that many have occupied the studio."

"For a number of years Monsieur Charnowski lived in your rooms. But he had luck. He became rich and famous. He moved into a fine apartment across the river. After him two young Englishmen moved in. But when their money was all spent and they had not learned to paint they went away. Since then the studio has been unoccupied."

"Perhaps I myself will be the next tenant," said Dayton. He hesitated a moment and then, smiling, but a little ill at ease——

"What has become of Claire D'Avril?" he asked. "I had to go away without saying good-by. I wrote many letters, but she never answered them."

"If you want to know what has become of her," said Madame Sidon, "you will have to make inquiries of the police. And very likely they will not be able to tell you. After you had gone away she disappeared for a while. Then she used to drop in once in a while to pose for Monsieur Charnowski."

"But he is a musician."

Madame Sidon shrugged her shoulders.

"He would draw and paint a little," she said "when it suited him."

Dayton could find nothing to say.

"After a while," said Madame Sidon, "she moved in bag and baggage. Then one fine day

she disappeared. I do not know what has become
of her. Monsieur Charnowski behaved like a
madman; to find her he spent money like water;
it was all in vain. Then success came to him,
and now he makes love to countesses and prin-
cesses. He has forgotten her."

It was then that Dayton ran up-stairs and let
himself into the studio. There was little furniture left but much dust. And yet it seemed to
him as if he had only been out for a walk; the
years fell from him, and a lump rose in his throat.
He had been very happy in that place. He felt
a little like Robin Hood returned to Sherwood
Forest. By pressing your face close to the bedroom window, and flattening yourself generally,
you could catch a glimpse of one of the bridges
over the Seine.

"It seems like yesterday," he thought, "and yet
how much water has flowed under the old bridge!"

Every now and then he drew a long breath
that resembled a sigh. He wondered why it was
that he had one judgment for himself and a judgment altogether different for other people. He
was sorry that Claire had come back to the studio
to keep house for another man. He ought to
have been glad. At least it proved that her heart
had not been broken. But he was not glad.

His Daughter

He fell to remembering with the utmost vividness details of their first meetings and of their subsequent life together. How sweet and gentle she had been—how loving and how forgiving! What jolly sprees they had had! He remembered days in the fields and under cool green trees, the little dinners at Gibier's; the sweet, cool cheek that she would lay against his when he was discouraged.

Then he remembered how they used to write messages and love-letters to each other and hide them under the loose tile in the hearth. He must have a look at that tile for old sake's sake. He felt for it with his foot; but the drifting dust of many years had enfirmed it so that it no longer rattled to the touch. He pried it out with the nail-file in his knife.

He blinked hard for a moment, for there was a letter under the tile.

He carried it to the light, his hand trembling. It was yellow and stained with damp. The writing was faded. The thick wad of money that he had placed in it for Claire was stained and yellow too.

He sat down weakly on the edge of a chair.

"She came back," he thought, "and I had gone, and she never looked under the tile!"

His Daughter

The pathos and the tragedy of that were very heavy and hard to bear. There was worse to follow. For, when he had returned the key to Madame Sidon and had turned to go, she called after him.

"There is something else," she said, "that perhaps you would like to know. Although you haven't asked."

"What is that, madame?"

"Claire D'Avril had a little girl born to her."

"When was that, madame?"

"Six or seven months after you went away."

It was not for some seconds that the amazement in his eyes yielded to horror.

"That was a long time ago," said the old woman, "but I supposed that you had your suspicions."

He shook his head numbly.

"And it may not have been yours."

If Madame Sidon had spoken the truth about the date of the child's birth there was no possible doubt as to the identity of the father. Dayton felt as if a great weight was crushing him down.

"I do not know what to say or do," he said. "What you have told me is horrible—horrible! What a brute she must have thought me—what a brute! See!" he cried, and he pulled the fa-

His Daughter

mous letter from his pocket and shook it in Madame Sidon's face. "The letter of explanation that I left for her, with my address, and money to take care of her until I could send her more! She never got it. She never looked under the loose tile in the hearth which we called our letter-box. She thought herself abandoned—abandoned!"

He paled upon the word, and after a wild glare at Madame Sidon turned and rushed out into the street. He walked in the direction of the river with long, furious strides. The light was failing and the cool air on his temples helped him to control himself.

In the middle of one of the bridges he halted and leaned against the parapet. His heart was beating furiously. And he felt as men at sea feel when they begin to think that the motion is going to affect them.

In his mind the images of his daughters were all mixed up; to picture that other daughter whom he had never seen he had only to think of his Ellen—the sheltered and protected Ellen; an Ellen abandoned by her father, poor, ill-nourished, abused, and whose mother perhaps had had to walk the streets for a living, was walking them at this very moment, perhaps—no longer very young

266

His Daughter

nor beautiful. . . . All that was tender in him and kind was stricken to the quick.

He looked at the palms of his hands and saw that his nails had made them bleed. And he wished that he had been struck dead before he had done any harm in the world.

A slender girl came loitering across the bridge. She paused when she came near Dayton.

"Bon soir, mon ami."

He looked up impatiently. But she saw more than the impatience in his face, and she made a little sound of pity, and with the swift direction of Frenchwomen——

"You are suffering?" she said.

"Yes," he said, "I am. That is true."

"We all have to suffer," said the girl, and she nodded to him and resumed her slow sauntering, but he called after her and she returned to him with the swift obedience and hopefulness of her class.

He was taking from his pocket an envelope from which bulged a thick wad of money.

"I shall suffer less," he said, "when I have given this to some one who needs it more than I do. I don't know how much there is, but quite a lot. Perhaps it will make your life a little easier for a while."

267

His Daughter

"But this is a fortune," she said.

"It is yours."

Her small, thin hands closed tightly on the money. He was drunk—of course. But what a cold, curious drunkenness!

"It will make my life a great deal easier, monsieur," said the girl, "if that is any pleasure to you."

"The pleasure of your saying that will have helped me a great deal. Good night, mademoiselle."

She hesitated.

"Monsieur—why stay here looking at the river? That is not good."

Dayton laughed harshly.

"Don't worry. Life isn't so easily settled; and, besides, if I jumped in the idea of death would frighten me, so that I would swim ashore. I am a coward."

He said this so fiercely that the girl shrank back. He turned his face once more to the river. And, except that he remembered having done something that had relieved the tension of his thoughts, she faded from his mind.

She stood for a little, watching his broad back, then shrugged her shoulders ever so little, turned, and sauntered on over the bridge. But as she reached the other side her pace quickened until it became a run. It was curious how the possession of much money could so lighten the spirit that one felt again like a little child.

He did not tell Dorothy that night. Indeed, he managed to pull himself together and give the ladies of his family an entertaining account of how he had spent the afternoon. It was not until Ellen had been kissed and sent to bed that he allowed his wife to perceive that there was something on his mind.

"Has Ellen a music lesson to-morrow?" he asked.

"Yes. Tuesdays and Fridays."

"I'd rather she didn't take from him any more. Anyway till I've had a talk with him."

"Have you heard something about him that you don't like?"

"Yes."

"Am I not to be told?"

"To-morrow, dear," said Dayton. "After I've talked with him I'll tell you all about everything."

He rose and, with one of those sudden, affectionate impulses which had helped Dorothy to forgive him for many injuries to her heart and pride, seated himself on the floor at her feet and rested his cheek against her knee.

With a certain hesitance and timidity she laid one hand on his thick hair and patted gently with the tips of her fingers. They did not speak. She was as happy as she could be. And that is to say that she was happy within reason and with reservations.

After quite a long time Dayton took the hand that rested on his head in his and kissed it—very reverently, as if it had been the hand of a saint.

"Is it possible, dear," he asked, "to begin life all over again?"

"It's always possible to try."

"I'm going to try."

The next morning Ellen was not feeling well. She had a slight headache and her temperature was a little above normal.

"Somehow I don't feel a bit worried about her," Dayton said, "but by all means have the doctor. I'll call on Charnowski at the time when Ellen was to have had her lesson. Then I'll be sure to find him."

Charnowski received Dayton with dignity and politeness. He regretted that Miss Ellen was indisposed. She had talent. It was curious how

His Daughter

Paris brought out the talent if only people had it in them.

"We've never met, I think," said Dayton.

"And yet we are not strangers. Madame your sister—eh, if it had not been for her cleverness and generosity I should never have got my start. I have for her almost more gratitude than my heart can contain."

Dayton bowed; then, looking Charnowski straight in the eyes——

"Monsieur Charnowski," he said, "please tell me anything that you can about Claire D'Avril."

Charnowski considered, chin in hand.

"Monsieur," he said presently, "I was once passionately jealous of you."

"You knew about me?"

"One had only to love that estimable girl," said Charnowski, "to realize that she had given her love to another—and for all time. It was very humiliating. She left me. She left for me a sad little note. And that was the end. I was frantic. I tried to trace her. But she had vanished like a soap-bubble. She left because—I will be very frank with you—the luck was not good. One night I was such a fool as to complain about expenses. I went out to keep a business appointment. I returned. She had gone. It was a

His Daughter

great pity. A great pity. For almost immediately the luck changed, and if she had stayed with me I could and would have given them everything."

"Them?" said Dayton in a numb voice.

Charnowski murmured: "I thought you knew."

"Until yesterday," said Dayton, "I did not suspect." He straightened himself and looked very brave and handsome.

"Monsieur," he said, "I wish you would tell me a little what my daughter was like."

"She was like her father, monsieur. She was like Miss Ellen—more fragile—but very like. She had also her talent for music; but hers, if I do not mistake the signs, was a prodigious talent. Only think—before she could even talk she would sit in my arms while I played for her, and then she would crow her pleasure and always she crowed on the right key!"

A lump was thickening in Dayton's throat. "How shall I find them?" he said simply. But there was a tragedy of appeal in his voice.

"I do not know," said Charnowski. "Such women as Claire—so affectionate, so gentle, so trusting, so unselfish—when they vanish it is like soap-bubbles. You know what life is like, however, as well as I do."

His Daughter

"It is an unbearable situation!"

"I too grieve over them sometimes," said Charnowski. "I have only one comfort: it was Claire who abandoned me."

"I do not know why I should care in what light I appear," said Dayton, "and yet in every man the impulse for self-justification is strong. This letter—it was filled with money—I found it yesterday under the tile in the hearth in the old studio. She never thought to look for it. And she thought that I had abandoned her!"

Charnowski smiled faintly and waved the letter aside.

"Often," he said, "I have felt with my foot that one of the tiles was loose, but I never thought to look under it."

Prosperity had removed from Charnowski's face its former sinister and hawklike character. If he was not a gentleman, he was a pretty good imitation of one. Dayton was surprised to find that he rather liked him, and he was inclined to let Ellen continue her lessons.

"I will keep my eyes and ears open," said Charnowski, "and, of course, if I see or hear anything I shall let you know. Do you know the chief of police? I will give you a card to him. It happens that, aside from being a very clever fellow, he is an excellent musician. He finds his way in here sometimes and I play for him."

"I'm obliged to you," said Dayton. "Is it worth while for my daughter to keep on with her music?"

"Distinctly."

Dayton was so wrapped up in his own thoughts that his feet carried him a block past his own door. It had seemed easy enough to tell Dorothy. It no longer seemed so. Still, after he had learned that Ellen was more comfortable, and sleeping, he told her the whole story from the beginning.

For the first time in his knowledge of her Dorothy looked stern and defensive and spoke without heart or justice.

"It will be better if it turns out that they are both dead," she said. "Do you want them both to come and live with us, or only the child?"

"Neither," said Dayton meekly. "I only thought that without robbing you and Ellen I could find enough money to make them comfortable and give the little girl a chance. When he told me that she looked like Ellen——"

Dorothy was softening.

"I'm sorry I said what I did."

274

His Daughter

"Any other woman would have said things long ago, and chucked me. . . . But, Dorothy, I've wronged them even more than I've wronged you. And I've got to try to make up to them, too. Haven't I?"

Dorothy drew a long breath.

"Yes, of course."

Dayton sent for a taxi and drove at once to the prefecture of police. And when he had been received by the chief he stated his business briefly.

"I remember the name very well," said the chief. "She figured in an inquest. Her lover was killed in an automobile accident. But that is many years ago. I will look into the matter. Will you call again—let us say a week from to-day?"

"That is very good of you. Is there anything that I can do to help?"

"Not the least thing." The chief laughed to himself when Dayton had gone.

"I have read of such things in their literature," he thought. "It is what they call the New England conscience. It does not prevent you from doing wrong things, but years afterward it assails you and makes you sorry that you have done them. Claire D'Avril. The thing made a noise at the time. The lover was an American, rich

and well known. She was left unprovided for
. . . so much I can remember in my own head."

Dayton returned to his apartment and learned
that Ellen was worse. Her temperature had risen
to a hundred and four. And the doctor was afraid
that she had typhoid.

Fear pierced Dayton like a cold, blunt knife.

VIII

WHEN a sufficient degree of suffering is reached even the feeblest demonstrations of affection become impossible. It was the setting in of this phenomenon in the case of Ellen that most wrung Dayton's heart and filled him with fear. She who had been the most responsive to his smile and to his voice of any human being had no longer the inclination or the power to respond.

She sank very rapidly. For forty-eight hours she had never a gleam of recognition for either her mother or her father. On the third day she lapsed into unconsciousness and died.

The blow to the Daytons was without any extenuating mercy whatever. They were not even so lucky as to be stunned by it. What they had lost, suffered, and were suffering, and must continue to suffer, was in every detail perfectly clear to them.

But all through they showed their breeding. Or else their grief was too great to be demonstrated by any outward manifestation. They went about the business of the burial clear-mindedly and with method. Dayton even secured the great Rodin to make a death-mask of the little girl. He even kept his appointment with the chief of police.

It was necessary to do these things or to go quite mad.

From the chief of police he was able to learn only that Claire D'Avril had changed her name and was no longer in Paris. The police of the great provincial cities were working on the case. The child, one of very many similarly situated, had presumably been boarded with a peasant family in Lorraine. The chief of police did not despair of finding her.

"Well," thought Dayton, as he drove back to the apartment, "God has this mercy—that he gives me these two unfortunates to think of, to find, and to provide for. And Charnowski says that the other looks like Ellen."

Before his eyes there arose a vision of Ellen's waxlike face, still and serene. "Only the other day," he thought, "she was coming to me as if to God; but now she has penetrated the great secret and has no more need of me."

Some of the time, as surely as he believed the facts of life, he believed that after death he would be reunited to his daughter in unutterable happi-

His Daughter

ness. It would be very different from the happiness that had been theirs on earth. There would be no fear of sickness, of partings. He would have no dire foreboding that some day she must grow up and love some one more than she loved him. She would have the same physical appearance—only the flesh thereof would be immortal and unchanging. Heaven—he believed that, having expiated by suffering, one went to heaven, and that there the memory of one's sins and shortcomings was taken away. And it was this fact that would make it heaven.

"Of this life I shall remember everything," he thought, "from the time she was born until the very moment before she got sick. Of my own life I shall remember only what was honorable and kind. I don't know how we shall occupy our time up there. But we shall be together. And Dorothy will be with us. And I shall have for her the feeling that I had when we knew that in a few hours Ellen was going to be born."

But at other times he had convictions about death that were very different. And then his deepest soul quivered with a horror and grief that were without comfort. For then he felt that he had forever parted from his daughter. And that when he, too, was dead, it would be as though their love for each other had never existed.

The gray hairs in his head increased in number. Physically and mentally he had aged many years in a few days.

The Daytons did not wish to leave Ellen always in France. So she was placed in the receiving-vault in the cemetery of Père la Chaise. Not until the next day did either of them have the faintest notion that the whole of Europe was about to be plunged in war.

Dayton's search for Claire D'Avril and for his other daughter ceased automatically. All the powers of France were mobilizing to fight for the nation's life. It never occurred to the Daytons to fly the country. The possibilities of doing war work seemed to them both a merciful dispensation. Dorothy at once offered her services to the Red Cross and became a nurse. Dayton for a time assisted Ambassador Herrick in sending hysterical Americans out of France, and then, after closing the apartment from which Dorothy had already been transferred to a base hospital, he joined an ambulance unit as a stretcher-bearer, and was sent almost at once to the front.

He had only a few minutes in which to say good-by to his wife. She looked tired; but there

His Daughter

was a light in her eyes that he had never seen before. She smelled of chloroform and iodoform. He had the taste upon his lips for a long time after kissing her.

"Yes," she admitted, "it's very hard work. And a good many of us are going to break down; but I'm not. The work will be easier when my muscles get trained to the heavy parts and when I get a little stiffened against suffering."

"I've been ordered to the front," said Dayton. "The risks, I imagine, will be very slight; but I've put the house in pretty good order. All the important papers are in Morgan Harjes's safe."

"You won't take risks 'that you don't have to?"

"You bet I won't!" He smiled innocently, but she knew that he was lying.

She sighed and looked him for a long time in the eyes.

"Fred," she said, "I've never stopped loving you. You know that."

"I know."

"I want you to come back to me. Only the firm belief that you are coming back to me, safe and sound, can keep me going."

"Oh, I'll turn up," he said, "like the bad penny that I am. Be sure of that!"

His Daughter

She put her hands on his shoulders.

"I've got to run," she said. "Good-by and God bless you!"

"And God bless *you*," came with the kiss that Dayton gave and received. And he was trembling with emotion, for he did not believe that they would ever meet again.

In his present state of mind he intended to get himself killed, if recklessness could manage it.

But of men who go down to battle with the avowed intention of getting themselves killed there are very few who zealously embrace the first opportunity which offers itself.

Dayton had not counted, perhaps, on being thrown with men who were almost recklessly alive, and almost idiotically anxious to go on living. Their high spirits, their pranks, their pretended ecstasies of fear, had an effect on him. Also the work was too much, the days too short, and the nights too well slept to afford him much opportunity for his private griefs. And the fact that he was rounding very quickly into splendid physical condition helped to heal the morbidity of his mind.

In those first days of the war the ambulance corps was not very well organized. It was, in addition, short of everything—short of ambulances,

His Daughter

short of stretchers, of men, and of medical supplies. It was the same with the field-hospitals—
with everything, indeed, except the steel-true
spirit and the national genius for fighting with
which the French armies went to war.

Dayton had imagined that his work would con-
sist chiefly in locating wounded men and carrying
them to the ambulance to which he was attached.
This, of course, after the battle was over, and
both Christian armies had called a sort of truce
in which to care for their wounded and to bury
their dead.

He had longed for death. He now found that
until the last invader was dead, mangled, or in a
strait-jacket, he had no wish to die.

Stretcher-bearing was not what he had imagined. It did sometimes and very simply assist
in helping to carry a wounded man from here to
there; but it was very much complicated by a
hundred and one complicated and nerve-racking
things that had to be learned from the beginning.

He learned to inject morphine into the wounded;
to have steady hands so that, when shells exploded in thunderous proximity, the needle should
not snap short off in the puncture. He learned
first aid—to locate and choke by pressure the sev-
ered arteries of men who otherwise must bleed to

death. He learned to know the signs of approaching dissolution, and to take and record the last whispered messages of the dying.

One *Macabre* night he worked with surgeons and nurses over a stream of wounded that was unending. A village church was the theatre. The wax candles had been taken from before the shrines of saints to throw a flickering light on the roughly improvised operating-tables.

Very early in the night the ether gave out and the chloroform. There was no morphine. But, just the same, abdominal cavities had to be cut open; legs and arms taken off; deep wounds caused by splinters of shells had to be ripped and slashed wide open with scissors to give infection an opportunity to drain off. Everything that is usually done under the merciful auspices of anæsthetics had to be done without. It was a night of horrible screaming, of torment that could not be endured.

Heavy men with powerful muscles, trained athletes, were needed to keep within bounds the awful struggles and galvanic jerkings of the wounded when their turn upon the table had come.

All night the shock and concussion of the contending cannon and the explosion of enemy

284

His Daughter

shells drew closer and closer. Sometimes, so great was the vibration, the bronze bell, high up in the belfry, could be heard musically mourning. Toward dawn the roof of the church opened with one terrible crash and a hellish orgy of white-hot light. One surgeon, three nurses, and one slightly wounded sergeant were killed instantly.

A flood of rain poured down through the hole in the roof. A second shell struck the church, and the great stained window over the high altar came down in tinkling dust. At that moment a surgeon was making some stitches, as fine and delicate as those which a good seamstress puts into a skirt. He did not even look up. He finished that which he was mending and put it back where it belonged. One of the nurses for that table stepped forward with a roll of bandages.

Another shell exploded against the side of the building, but still the surgeons' work went on, the work of the nurses, and the travail of the hurt. They were like dogs: they howled from the pain, but between spasms they sought with trusting and loving looks for the faces of those who, in order to save them, tormented them.

The hands of the surgeons were cramped. Their forearms ached. The nurses looked like

His Daughter

butchers. Dayton, exerting all of his remaining strength to hold an amputation case in position, resembled one of those straining and terrible figures which Michelangelo used to hew from a block of marble.

Then word came to evacuate the church. The spire was tottering. The roof was no longer safe. Many of the wounded could not be moved. A shell exploded in the choir and set fire to the wooden stalls. A bedding of straw, damped with blood, caught and the church was soon filled with a blinding, choking smoke. The roar of the fire could be heard above the roar of the guns.

There had not been time to carry all the wounded from the building. It was impossible to go back into that place of fire and smoke, of glass that crashed from the stained windows as the leads melted—into the hell from which there still issued the screams and howlings of those who had been condemned in the flesh through no fault of their own. . . .

Stretcher-bearing was by no means the simple, methodic business that Dayton had anticipated.

In the grief and anguish of thousands he came very soon to forget that there had been such a person as Frederick Dayton and that the said person had thought himself unhappy and ill used

His Daughter

—had, indeed, gone through a private crucifixion of his own.

There were too many mothers and sweethearts in these wrecked French villages who, having lost all that was dear to them, still faced life with calm cheerfulness and the passionate desire to be of service, for Dayton to dwell upon his own Ellen's passing with anything but serenity.

It was impossible that so many thousands of lovers could have been parted forever. And he was very sure that after service and sacrifice and smoke and fire, and a death perhaps of anguish, he would one day be with his darling again.

Then followed the terrible days of the Marne, when General Joffre, staking all that makes life worth living upon his will to conquer, ordered those of his men who could to advance, and those who could not to die where they stood. At the end of those days, as all men know, the invaders were sent staggering back in defeat, and England was given time and opportunity to prepare for war.

A strip of ravished Lorraine was won back by the French, and through its ruined villages, thick as plums in a rich pudding, Dayton, as opportunity offered and the exigencies of the service permitted, sought for his daughter.

His Daughter

He had little to go on, and his search was without luck. Once, in the village of Bois Dormis, he was very close to her, but she had her back turned and a shawl over her head, and the ambulance was not making any halt, so that he did not, at that time, discover her identity. And, indeed, for some time now his inquiries had been growing more and more perfunctory; so many of the young people had left the villages of their own accord, so many had been carried off by the Germans. At times he despaired of ever finding his daughter.

The more he learned about the Germans, the more he longed to hurt them, and he succeeded in getting himself transferred from the ambulance to an aviation school somewhere in the south of France.

Six months later he was back in Lorraine, a member of a small escadrille, a pilot of promise.

Through his own sufferings and the sufferings of others he had become cold as ice, cold as the eagles who soar in the zenith searching with cruel telescopic eyes for carrion in the world below.

Once free from the earth it never occurred to Dayton that he could be hurt. It was the golden opportunity to hurt Germans that occupied him.

His Daughter

You could hurt them in many ways. You could locate a battery or a supply-train and direct upon them destructive French cannon-fire. You could, stealing up in the cover of a cloud, shut off the loud crackling motor and coast down suddenly and at frightful speed upon a company of soldiers, spray them with a stream of lead from your machine-gun, turn on your power, and, rising and receding more swiftly than an eagle, disappear once more into the asylum of the clouds.

One day he brought down a German fighting-plane, and was thereafter decorated by a French general and kissed upon both cheeks. One day his machine was riddled through and through by shrapnel bullets and the motor put out of commission. He himself was untouched, and, by cold, clear thinking, regained control of his falling plane and made a safe descent. Two hours later, having worked over the crippled motor with his two mechanics until the sweat poured from them, he was flying again.

The airmen are the lords of the French villages. They are the old knights come to life again to battle for France. They are a race apart. There is none to say them nay. It was one thing for a stretcher-bearer to hunt through the ruined villages for a lost daughter. It was quite another when a knight of the air said that one was lost whom he greatly wished should be found.

One of Dayton's mechanics, Dumal, was from the little town of St. Nicholas du Port. He was a wise and observant youth, and one in whom his superiors had great confidence.

"My friend," said Dayton to him one day, "about thirteen or fourteen years ago a young woman brought her child to Lorraine and put her to board with a family in one of the little villages. I do not know which village nor the name of the family, nor the name of the little girl—she was little more than a baby. I know only the name of the mother; and I *could* supply the name of the father, only it would not be of any help."

"You wish to find the little girl, monsieur?"

"Yes."

Dumal wore a discreet expression.

"The name of the mother, monsieur?"

"Claire D'Avril."

Dumal wrote the name on a loose leaf of his note-book. And strictly to himself he observed: "Such things *will* happen even in the best families." Aloud he said:

"Can it be known that it is you, monsieur, who seek?"

"That would not help in any way."

His Daughter

"On the contrary, the peasants will put themselves out for an aviator as they would not for any ordinary person."

Dayton knew this to be true.

"Very well, then," he said. "Let my name appear in the affair. That is nothing, if the child can be found. What do you propose to do?"

"To speak of what monsieur desires to a few peasants. Within a week monsieur's wishes will be known to every peasant in Lorraine. Electricity is wonderful, monsieur. But the people who live close to the ground are still more wonderful."

Ten days later Dumal knocked on the door of Dayton's room in the coquettish château where the escadrille was quartered. Dayton looked up impatiently. He was working on a new range-finder for airplanes. When he saw the expression on Dumal's face his impatience left him. Dumal might have stood for a statue of mind triumphing over matter. He attempted (and failed) to speak in a matter-of-fact voice.

"She lives in Bois Dormis," he said. "She keeps house for the curé, who is a very old man. He has taught her Latin and geography, and already she was the organist in the village church until the Germans blew the roof in and the rains have ruined the organ. The old doctor is also

His Daughter

her friend. Jointly he and the curé have been her guardians ever since the death of the foster-parents. She has the same name as the mother, Claire D'Avril; that is why it has been not impossible to find her, and she is very beau-tiful."

Dayton was very deeply moved. Presently he said: "The Germans—they were in Bois Dormis?"

"Yes, monsieur; but so was the old doctor, and so was the old curé. No harm came to her. Only fancy, monsieur, this old doctor is quite a scientist. He has in his house objects of great scientific interest; among others there is, for instance, a large stuffed crocodile. From this curious beast, on the approach of the Germans, monsieur, our droll doctor removes the stuffing, punctures the hide with breathing holes, and for the stuffing substitutes—the young lady. The neighbors speak of her as 'Our Little Lady of the Crocodile. . . .' Among the young women of Bois Dormis, monsieur, Mademoiselle Claire D'Avril was one of them to escape. . . . That is a fair percentage, when you consider that it is a very little village. . . ."

Dayton interrupted almost brusquely, so great was his excitement.

"The fog," he exclaimed. "Does it lift at all?"

His Daughter

"If monsieur is willing to fly low, the conditions are not altogether bad."

"How far is Bois Dormis?"

"A hundred and thirty-two kilometres."

"You know the way? Good! Get the car out of the hangar. You accompany me."

"I thank you," said Dumal. He was sincere. What he had heard concerning "Our Little Lady of the Crocodile" had immensely excited his interest.

It was one of those days, all too frequent, which the devil seems to spew up for the protection of the invading armies. You could not fly against the enemy; for if you flew high enough to stand a chance with his anti-aircraft equipment, you flew among clouds and mists, so that his trenches, guns, positions, and movements of munitions were completely hidden from you. On such days the airmen are not sent out, and they do as they please.

Flying low, however, the landmarks of the country were mistily visible, and, roaring at top-speed, Dayton's tiny plane picked up, one by one and very swiftly, the steeples, the hills, and the bridges which, like blazed trees in a forest, marked the airway to Bois Dormis.

His Daughter

With a graceful half-turn, such as a plover makes when it sets its wings to light on a sandbar, Dayton landed in the midst of a dew-drenched pasture.

His progress across the field was slow. Wooden crosses and low mounds marked the graves of French soldiers who had died for their country. At each grave custom and the reverence in his heart compelled Dayton to halt, to bring his heels together with a sharp click, and to salute deliberately. Dumal, hard at his master's heels, imitated him exactly.

They did not speak until they were in the village.

"That will be a hard field to plough," said Dayton.

"It will be best to put a fence about each grave," said Dumal, "and let the cattle graze between. This village was taken and retaken many times."

Of the fifty-odd houses which had composed the red-roofed village of Bois Dormis, only that of the doctor remained entirely habitable. The village was a shambles of blackened limestone, of tumbled brick chimneys, of twisted iron bedsteads. Of the church there stood only the four walls. The roof had fallen in and the spire had followed. But where old gardens had not been buried too

His Daughter

deep with débris were patches of bright color; and among these roses and perennials old peasant women were weeding and watering just as if nothing had happened.

Hard by the church stood the curé's house. A noble pear-tree, pruned and trained to the last inch, had once covered the whole of the front; but some highly cultured Teuton had hacked through the thick trunk which sprouted from the ground at the right of the front door, so that the loving care of a hundred years had never a leaf to show.

Dayton knocked upon the door and it was almost instantly opened by the curé. To that one people came with their troubles at all hours of the day and night, and he never kept them waiting.

"My friend," said Dayton to Dumal, "come back in an hour."

Then he went into the house with the curé.

"I have come," said Dayton, "to see Claire D'Avril."

His voice was trembling. So were his knees. The eagle had lost his coldness.

"She will return presently," said the curé. "She does our cooking next door. We lost our kitchen and our scullery in the last bombardment. . . . You are not well. Please sit down. I have

His Daughter

here a bottle of cognac. Perhaps a little glass would do us both good."

The old man fetched the cognac and two little glasses from a carved walnut cabinet, dusted the neck of the bottle with a clean napkin, and filled the glasses.

He was very thin and frail, the color of a wax candle. He was over eighty; but he had perfect vision and his black eyes had all the fire and valor of youth.

Dayton gulped down the brandy. Then he spoke.

"My father," he said, "this is a very solemn moment in my life. Claire D'Avril is my daughter. It is only within the year that I have learned of her existence. I have come in order that I may undo, as much as is possible, the evil that I have done."

"The evil is not beyond remedy, perhaps," said the curé. "You are a Protestant?"

"But I have often thought that I should like to confess my sins to a good man—like yourself. I do not know the forms. May I tell you how Claire D'Avril happens to be in this world, and how it happens that I seem to have abandoned her and her mother before her?"

The old curé nodded and, leaning forward, his

chin in his hand, listened. There was only one interruption.

Fingers tapped upon the door that led into the next room, and the curé called out: "Don't come in at this moment. I am receiving a confession."

"That was she?" asked Dayton.

The curé nodded, and Dayton went on with his story, concealing nothing, to the end. Then the curé smiled his gentle, wise old smile. "I have listened to worse things, my son," he said, "and your repentance seems to me full and without flaw. If you had not sinned our little Claire would not have existed. She has lived a happy life, and she has made many others happy."

"Her mother?" Dayton asked.

"Of her own accord," said the curé, "she renounced the child many years ago. The life she had been obliged to lead had rendered her unfit in her own eyes to enjoy the privilege of being a mother. The last time she came, and that is many years ago, the neighbors suspected her for what she was. . . . All this is very tragic. In many ways I have never known a better woman."

"What has become of her?"

"I do not know. But it may be that, through renunciation and self-sacrifice, she has found happiness. In my youth," he continued, "I was very sharp with sinners, but in later years more lenient. But you have confessed, and I am to impose a penance—is that your desire?"

"Why, yes. If you can think of any penance which will make for expiation."

"To the mother," said the old man, "you have a very obvious duty—if you can find her. That duty is, of course, purely financial. A greater duty is to your own wife. It is not possible for you to love her as she deserves to be loved. But at least a clever man, whose heart is in the right place, can always make the woman who loves him believe that he loves her. I give you this penance: to find me Claire D'Avril's mother, if that is possible, and to make her as comfortable as may be for the rest of her life; to reunite with your own wife in a true marriage. You are not too old to hope for children to take the places of those which you have lost——"

"But I have only lost my Ellen——"

The curé shook his head.

"Will you, my son, by disclosing yourself, disturb the simple, sane ideas and the real happiness of many years' standing? You cannot take Claire with you into your world—a thousand things forbid. And if, in that sweet-tempered mind, there is any room for discontent, would you

His Daughter

be the means of putting it there? . . . Here with us, in spite of all our shortcomings and narrowness, she has been happy. She will continue to be as happy as it is right to be in these evil days. . . . My son, I have indicated the penance."

"But," exclaimed Dayton, "she is flesh of my flesh—bone of my bone!"

"If she were other, there could be no penance in renouncing her. . . . Do you find no wisdom in what I have said to you, my son?"

"Wisdom, father, yes. But also pain that is almost intolerable. . . . I am rich, father——"

"She has never felt the want of money."

"I would love her as no one else could."

"She was a delicate baby when she first came to Bois Dormis," said the curé gently. "In our pleasant country air she grew strong. There is no longer any stiffness in her arm. . . . It resulted from some sickness of childhood. Our good doctor cared for her body. Twice a year he took her to the American dentist in Nancy. I cared for her soul. Between us we have cared for her mind. The man who is so fortunate as to marry her will have the best housekeeper and the best bookkeeper in Lorraine. Even in the great world of music she would be a success. But she does not know that. You were speaking of the superior

299

sort of love that you could give her. There is an honest boy of this country who loves her very dearly, and she loves him in the same way. When this cruel war is over they are to be married."

"He is in the army ?"

"Of course."

"And you think I should only interfere with their happiness ?"

"It is best that they work out their destiny in the station of life to which they are accustomed and to which they are attached."

"At least, my father, let me recompense you for all that she has cost."

"Can you give me back the fifteen years of devotion that I have given her? You cannot. I would not take it back if you could."

"Will you accept from me a new roof for your church, and a new spire?"

"Willingly, my son."

Dayton's head dropped forward in deep reflection.

"Could I see her?" he asked presently. "I will promise not to reveal myself."

"You are only making your penance harder."

"It will be no harder than I deserve."

"Very well, then," said the curé, "you shall have your wish."

His Daughter

He stepped to the door which led to the adjoining room, opened it, and in a caressing voice:

"Claire, my dear," he said, "a glass of water, if you please, for the American aviator."

She came presently carrying a great white-and-gold pitcher and a tumbler. The fashion of her dress was lost upon Dayton. He saw only her face and her eyes. She resembled Ellen as one pansy resembles another.

He had risen, and his hand trembled as he lifted the tumbler of water to his lips.

"I thank you," he said.

"Don't mention it, monsieur," she said. And she had an odd quality of Ellen's voice, a certain deep and tranquil quality that ripped and tore his heart-strings.

"Our hero," said the old curé, who was watching Dayton very closely, "has flown far and fast. It takes muscle to fly. See, my dear, how his hands tremble!"

And he laughed quietly. Dayton put the offending hands behind his back.

"The good father," he said, "tells me that you are engaged to be married."

"*Oui*, monsieur. It is true."

"Do you love each other very much?"

His Daughter

She only smiled serenely and looked him in the eyes.

"You would rather have him than anything else you can think of—riches—fine clothes—motors—jewels——"

"Tell him not to tease me," she appealed to the curé; "he thinks I am a child."

Dayton felt as if he was standing by an open grave. He smiled crookedly.

"My father," he said, "put just a drop of the brandy in this water. I have got to go, and up there in the fogs and mists it is very cold, and everything is uncertain."

When the door had closed upon Dayton, Claire D'Avril stood looking at it for some moments.

"He appeared very much moved, the American," she said presently.

"Not so long ago," said the curé, "he lost his only child. Doubtless you reminded him of her. . . . His name is Dayton. He has a good heart. . . . I shall mention him sometimes in my prayers."

"Very well, then," said Claire D'Avril, "so will I, if it's the proper thing to do. And besides, there was something about him that touched me."

Dayton had been admitted to the doctor's house.

His Daughter

Dumal waited in the broken village street. The doctor was as old as the curé, and like him he was alert and keenly alive.

"I have a favor to ask," said Dayton; "I wish to see the crocodile in which you hid Claire D'Avril from the Germans."

"With pleasure, Monsieur l'Aviateur. This way."

The famous crocodile lay along the end wall of the doctor's museum; it was very old, and broken in places.

"At night," said the doctor, "we let her out, so that she could stretch herself and breathe freely. This rent was made by a drunken soldier with his bayonet. He thought the beast was alive. It missed her by a finger's breadth."

Dayton knelt by the dusty crocodile, and broke down completely. He sobbed and cried like a little child.

The doctor watched him, chin in hand.

"I guessed who he was from the resemblance," he thought, "and now I know."

He laid a firm hand on Dayton's shoulder.

"You have told her who you are?"

Dayton shook his head. Gradually the sobs ceased, and he rose totteringly to his feet.

"I am not to tell her," he said, "ever. That is

His Daughter

part of the penance. . . . Forgive me for making a fool of myself, but God gave me two daughters, my friend, and within the year I have buried them both."

Presently, his jaws set, his nerves in iron control, his heart beating quietly, he was once more scudding through the low-hanging mists. The next day was bright and clear, and Dayton, ten thousand feet above the troubles of this earth, met an enemy aviator and in fair fight slew him.

The next day his own machine was crumpled by a burst of shrapnel. As Dayton neared the ground back of the French lines flames burst from his gasolene-tank and followed him like the tail of a comet.

When they snatched him from the wreckage his clothes had begun to burn, and the blood that gushed from a wound in his right breast sputtered and hissed as it became steam.

IX

ABOVE the forest floated a great Red Cross flag. Its flagpole, however, was not attached to a hospital, but to a tree, and served as a sort of rallying-point for the farthest-flung German shells.

The hospital itself, a coquettish Louis XVIth château, carried no dangerous distinguishing marks. Its roof, indeed, was gravelled and painted to represent paths and flower-beds, so that to the passing air pirate, on murder bent, the building resembled a part of the large garden in which it stood.

Only very sick men were taken to that hospital; men too sick to be carried by train to the more luxurious and better-equipped base hospitals. It was a life-or-death sort of place. In the old gardens, since they had been cultivated and loved for generations, the digging was good, and there were almost as many white wooden crosses as rose-trees.

The garden was enclosed by a tall wall of stone, plastered over. Fruit-trees trained against the wall resembled a charming collection of ladies'

His Daughter

fans. At each corner of the garden was a round tower with a candle-snuffer top.

Dorothy had fallen in love with the place, and she hoped that when the war was over she might be able to buy it. Under the gravelled and painted roof war had lost its horror for her, and she had known peace. The sufferings patiently borne and the deaths gallantly encountered had immensely broadened her grasp of life—its meanings, its splendors, and its futilities.

"But for this war," she sometimes thought, "humanity might have rotted away and left no record to prove that at heart it is noble."

The garrison, if I may so call them, of that hospital were picked men and women. They had been graduated, so to speak, from the base hospitals because of their peculiar fitness, their strength, skill, and courage.

The chief surgeon was only twenty-seven years old. He had the same sort of character that men should have who command armies or dreadnaughts. Short of equipment and supplies, he performed miracles in the improvised and not well-lighted operating-theatre.

The nurses represented various classes of society. The money-spending class, if I must not say the aristocratic class, was represented by

His Daughter

Dorothy herself and the young Duchess of Tours. There were the wife of a clerk in the government service, two deep-chested, indomitable peasant women from the neighborhood, and among others a woman who, in spite of a certain gentleness and sweetness of manner, looked as if she had suffered almost as much as she had lived.

Even in her Red Cross costume Adèle Soubisse looked as if she were playing a part. Her face was thin and deeply lined; she had the kind of skin that women who paint their faces develop during an illness when they no longer care how they look. Her hair had once been bleached or dyed a bright yellow; but since the last application of the dye the hair had grown nearly three inches, and these three inches were a deep red splashed with gray.

But the only questions asked in that hospital concerning a nurse were these: "Is she strong?" "Can she bandage?" "In short, does she know her business?"

Among all the nurses no one was more skilful then Adèle Soubisse. Therefore her somewhat obvious past was very properly ignored, and even that highborn and fastidious lady the Duchess of Tours treated her as an equal.

The little Ford ambulance hurried up the drive, past the pond with the swans, and through the

His Daughter

plantation of lilacs, as fast as its faithful little engine could carry it.

The driver and his stretcher-bearer extracted from the back, not without difficulty because of the weight, a stretcher on which lay a very big man covered to the eyes with a blanket.

The driver and the stretcher-bearer carried him into the receiving-room of the hospital, and a few moments later emerged with the empty stretcher, slipped it back into its rack, and drove recklessly away.

The orderlies undressed the wounded man in a very swift and businesslike way. They simply cut his clothes off with scissors. They washed him all over with soap and water, dried him, lifted him to a sterile stretcher, and carried him at once to the operating-room. The chief surgeon was waiting. And so the wounded man was lifted at once from the stretcher to the operating-table.

Dorothy Dayton happened to be on duty. When the surgeon started to pull down the sheet and she saw the face of the wounded man, she screamed and for the first time in her life fainted dead away. The surgeon did not turn his head.

"Take Mrs. Dayton away and send the Soubisse to take her place."

When Adèle Soubisse saw the face of the

His Daughter

wounded man she too had the impulse to scream, but she managed to control herself. The hand with which she picked up the chloroform cone trembled, however, and the surgeon exclaimed:

"What's the matter with the women to-day?"

So saying he dipped a great sponge in iodine and slathered it widely over the wounded man's chest.

"He has been burned too," he said, "but not badly."

While the wounded man inhaled the chloroform he grew icy cold, and they wrapped his legs and abdomen in hot blankets. And the surgeon consulted a ticket which had come with the wounded man, like an invoice with a consignment of goods: "One-half grain morphine—anti-tetanus serum—landed with great violence—may have inhaled flames—I think not—possible internal injuries."

He laid the ticket down, washed and scrubbed his hands and forearms for the last time, selected a pair of curved scissors from a sterilizing tray, and attacked the gorgeous form of youth and genius.

The scissors clicked and rasped savagely, and the round hole in the wounded man's breast began to open like some horrible dark-crimson flower.

At that moment Dorothy Dayton returned to

the post of duty. She reached out her hand to take the chloroform cone from Adèle Soubisse, but the woman with the unsavory past shook her head.

"He's my husband," protested Mrs. Dayton.

"All the more reason why a—a comparative stranger, whose nerves will not give way, should be in attendance," said Adèle Soubisse.

"Stop quarrelling, ladies," exclaimed the surgeon, "or else I shall execute the judgment of Solomon. I shall cut this poor fellow in two and give you each half!"

Dayton presently, his wound draining and bandaged, his burns paraffined, was carried to a bed in the main ward. But both Dorothy and Adèle Soubisse remained in the operating-room. Another case had arrived and was ready to go on the table, and the ordinary routine nursing in the wards had to be left in less skilful hands.

It speaks well for the discipline that comes from continued self-sacrifice that Dorothy Dayton made no plea to be allowed to nurse her husband. Her duty, and she knew it well, was to the amputation case that was being laid on the operating-table, one foot dangling and the other blown clean off. If Dayton was going to die, even, it

His Daughter

was her duty not to be with him during his last minutes, if during those minutes some other badly wounded man had need of her skill.

All day badly hurt men came dribbling into the hospital, for there had been a battle, but toward dusk the last one had been bandaged and put to bed and Dorothy Dayton and Adèle Soubisse had their first opportunity to visit the main ward to which Dayton had been taken.

But there was nothing that they could do. He was either asleep or unconscious. It was difficult to detect any rise and fall of the broad, deep chest.

They turned away presently and had a look at all the others who had "passed over the table" that day, and then, by common accord, they slipped bareheaded into the garden and strolled side by side, breathing long breaths of the sweet air and ridding their lungs and clothes of the aftermath of chloroform.

"You are very brave," said Adèle Soubisse presently. "For I can see that you love him very much."

"He is all that I have in the world," said Dorothy simply. "We lost our little girl."

"That is hard. I also lost my little girl. But not in the same way. I gave her up so that she might never be ashamed of me. Yes, life is very hard."

"I used to think so," said Dorothy. "But you and I have both seen misfortunes by the side of which our own seem of little account. When every one is so brave it is not easy to be a coward."

"Monsieur Dayton was in the aviation?"

"At first he was with an ambulance; but men do not like to be regarded as non-combatants."

"This pesky hair of mine!" exclaimed Adèle Soubisse. A loop had come loose and fallen forward over one eye. "It's a wonder people don't laugh whenever they see me. But at one time yellow was all the fashion. . . ." She patted the loop back into place and fastened it with a pin. "It was very foolish of me, for the original color was not really half-bad."

"What made you change?" Dorothy asked.

"Oh, madame, people like me—we have our popularity to think of. One feels that one is getting old—the hair-dresser guarantees a certain effect—and behold we are disfigured beyond repair. . . . Dinner ought to be ready. . . . Shall we see how your husband is getting on? . . . I too feel a great interest in him. . . . A thousand years ago I thought that I was going to be married to a man who resembled him."

His Daughter

"And what happened, Adèle ?"

"He left me, madame."

They walked in silence through the darkening garden.

"What did you say, Adèle ?"

"Did I say something ? I must have been thinking aloud. After him, I was thinking, the deluge ! But every one is kind here. People now are only interested in what a woman can do —not in what she has done."

Once more they stood beside Dayton.

"All right ?" Dorothy asked the nurse who had charge of him.

"He wakened two hours ago and asked for a little water. He is stronger, I think. It is good for him to sleep."

The occupant of the corner bed was hidden from view by a common Japanese-paper screen. As they passed out on the way to the dining-room Dorothy Dayton bowed her head and Adèle Soubisse crossed herself. For that paper screen, with its flight of white herons against a background of snow-capped Fuji, meant that a man's work in this world was over and that a soul was passing on.

"It is the amputation case," said Adèle when they were outside. "He had lost too much blood."

His Daughter

During the night Dayton waked again and asked for water. After that he was fretful and restless. Dorothy had asked to be called and presently she was bending over him.

His mouth quivered.

"Is it so bad?" he whispered.

"It isn't bad at all," said Dorothy decidedly. "It's just an accident that I happen to be here. I'm on duty in this hospital."

The wounded man nodded a number of times.

"I remember now," he said. "I asked to be brought here. This is Deux Fontaines. But I had forgotten."

"Are you comfy?"

"Now I've got you."

She got a basin of water and from a sponge squeezed cool water repeatedly over his wrists and hands.

"That's *good*," he said several times. "That's good!"

There was a long silence. She hoped that he would fall asleep. But there was something on his mind.

"I found her, Dorothy," he said.

"The little girl? I'm glad. But we'll not talk about things until you are stronger."

His Daughter

"I am not to see her any more," he said. A few tears oozed out of his eyes and ran down his cheeks. Then he said: "It doesn't matter. I have you."

Holding her hand with a surprising show of strength, he abandoned himself to sleep.

When she returned to her dormitory, which she shared with Adèle Soubisse, and which during the daytime was occupied by two of the night nurses, she found Adèle sitting up in bed and eager for the news.

"All right?" she asked.

"Yes," said Dorothy gently, "he's reached the little-child stage."

"They all do when the shock begins to affect them."

"It's good of you to take so much interest, Adèle. It makes everything so much easier for me."

She slipped into bed and after a little tossing slept.

Not so Adèle Soubisse; for she had that within her heart which defied sleep and solace. She lay flat upon her back staring into the dark; one hand clutched at the region above her heart, the other was clinched so that the short nails made deep dents in the palm. "O God," she thought, "have

315

His Daughter

a little pity; for I feel toward him just as I used
to feel when I was Claire D'Avril!"

No new cases came in, and the chief surgeon
was having late breakfast and cigarettes in the
garden. It was here that Adèle Soubisse found
him. She sat down on the bench beside him and
he made her accept a cup of coffee. He had a
special coffee for himself; it was very bad, but he
was very proud of it.

"Well, Adèle," he said, with a laugh, "is it for
this morning, the story of your life? You know
you promised for that important book which I
am to write some day."

"I am actually going to tell you something,"
said Adèle. "But first, monsieur, I wish you to
find some one to take my place."

"Impossible. You are too familiar with my
ways. I can't spare you."

"It is because of Madame Dayton and her
husband," said Adèle. "You have often asked
me for the story of my life. Very well, I will tell
you the beginning. The beginning was Monsieur
Dayton."

"You do not wish him to recognize you?"

"It isn't that. She—she has been very good
to me. We have shared the same room, the same

·hours. Never by word or sign has she made me feel that there is any difference between us. She is an angel!"

"And you? You are not an angel?"

Adèle Soubisse couldn't help laughing at that. The surgeon smote the arm of the bench with his fist.

"And I say you are," he exclaimed. "I say there is no better woman in France, and when I say that I am speaking in terms of angels."

"I could not bear to be the cause of hurting her."

"Seriously," said the surgeon, "it seems to me that you have only to keep away from him. Then, if that isn't satisfactory—well, you deserve something, and I will see what can be done."

"I thank you with all my heart," she said. Adèle Soubisse finished her coffee.

"Sometimes," she said, "I think the war was sent so that whole peoples might redeem their sins. Surely the pasts of those who have served, fought, and died will be forgiven."

"I am told," said the surgeon, "that you may leave your money on a bench in Montmartre and find it there when you return."

"And after the war," said Adèle, "it will not be necessary to go back to the old way of making a living."

His Daughter

"There will be plenty of honest work for every one."

"Hitherto it has never been like that."

"What shall you do when the war is over?"

"I shall continue to be a nurse, if I may."

Secretly Adèle Soubisse believed that after many years of redemption she might be considered fit to associate with her daughter.

Two days later the surgeon told her that he had found a place for her and some one to take her place. "To-morrow morning," he said, "the inspector-general will bring the new nurse and will take you to the hospital with which the exchange has been arranged."

Late that night, while Dorothy Dayton slept soundly, Adèle Soubisse rose stealthily, dressed in the dark, and went down to the main ward to see Dayton for the last time.

She stood for a while looking at him and thinking of old times. Then she bent swiftly and touched his hand with her lips. But he was not, as she had supposed, asleep. He opened his eyes on the instant.

In the dim light his pupils were widely extended, so that in the white face the eyes looked like two pools of ink. She could not withhold an exclamation of love and pity commingled, and

His Daughter

she was turning to make her escape when he caught her hand.

"I'm not dreaming?" he whispered; "it is you?"

The wounded men in the adjoining beds slept soundly. Having assured herself of this, Adèle Soubisse knelt by Dayton's bed and whispered:

"Yes. It's I."

Their conversation was all in whispers.

"I have hurt you terribly," he said; "but, Claire, when I went away I left a letter for you and money."

"I never received it."

"You never looked for it. It was under the tile in the hearth. Only the other day I visited the studio and looked, and there it was. But I wrote many letters."

"I never received them."

"But you believe that I wrote them?"

"Yes."

"You have had a hard life?"

"Yes."

"Listen, Claire; I have seen our daughter. They told me of your sacrifice, and the curé insisted that I should make the same sacrifice. In addition he told me that I must find you, and provide for you."

His Daughter

She shook her head.

"I am well provided for," she said. "I have work to do."

"You are one of the staff in this hospital ?"

"I go to-morrow to another."

"Why ?"

"Does it matter ?"

"Is it because of me ?"

"It is because of your wife."

"But I have told her about you."

"I do not wish to be identified. We have shared and shared alike—the same room—the same hours. I love her very much."

"But I wish to do something for you."

"If I am ever in trouble I will write to you. I have an address which will always reach Madame Dayton. We have promised to correspond."

She laughed softly.

"I couldn't go without seeing you once more," she said, "but I did not mean to wake you. You are better ? Everything is all right ?"

"I am going to get well, but it will be slow."

"You will not fly any more ?"

"As soon as they will let me. . . . How else could I get my sins forgiven ?"

"There are sins ?"

"I have not been a faithful husband. I have

320

made a great deal of trouble in the world. But since the war I have no desire except to save France and to redeem myself in my own eyes."

"It is the same with me."

"Claire—is there nothing I can do—nothing that you wish me to do? I have never thought of you with anything but tenderness and compunction."

"You can do one thing. It is only to answer a question."

"I will answer it."

"If you had known that there was going to be a child . . . ?"

"I would have married you."

"Truly?"

"Truly."

She drew a long breath of relief. "I have always thought that," she said, "and that thought has kept me going through some hard times."

"I don't think I understand."

"It is very simple. I loved you very much. And the only thing that made life possible was believing that you would have taken good care of me if you had only known."

The wounded man in the next bed thrashed nervously.

"We've disturbed him," she said. "I must go."

His Daughter

She bent very close and whispered:

"Good-by, and good luck. I have never stopped loving you."

With swift gentleness she freed her hand from his and stole softly away. They never saw each other again.

"Dorothy dear," wrote Dayton, "the day's news has made us all very happy. Gurton of the escadrille made us all laugh at breakfast. He came up to me and stared at me until I thought he was crazy. I asked him what the matter was, and he said: 'America has declared war, and I'm practising looking people in the face again.' We all feel like that. Things had gotten so shameful that they simply couldn't be explained any more.

"Of course America can't start right in and do things. She is no better prepared to fight than she was the day the Germans fired on Liège. That's a hard thing to believe; but it's a fact and there's no use crying about it. For the present what counts is the moral effect; and if the Allies can hang on for another twelve months there will be material effects of real importance.

"The situation just now is touch and go. Russia is obviously shot to pieces; France is beginning to fail in man-power, and so far no real retort courteous has been found for the submarine. But I refuse to borrow too much trouble on that score. It will be a tight squeeze, but we're going to win. If we don't—then the quicker the name of America is forgotten the better. Perhaps the *Lusitania* and all the other outrages were not a sufficient cause of war; at least they should have been a sufficient cause to make us prepare for war; and if civilization takes a licking the fault will be with America. When I think that we might so easily have at this moment a couple of million men trained and equipped and ready to be shipped over, and that, roughly speaking, we haven't a darn thing, it makes me sick.

"I brought down my fourth German yesterday, and have been mentioned again in the Order of the Day. I didn't see him fall; but when I'd circled to have another go at him he'd disappeared.

"Things are very active up this way. We fly four or five times a day, weather permitting, and the cannon never stop. We live in a dreary barracks, which leaks, and being an airman is not the lordly job it used to be.

"It will be good when this war is over and we can be together again. I think about you almost

all the time. I am to have eight days' leave next
month and I will spend them in the nearest village so that I can see you every day.

"Your loving husband,

"F. D."

About the future Dayton was very sanguine.
He had been through the fire, and he felt that he
was an instrument which had been tempered and
could be counted on. He believed that Dorothy
still loved him and that God would permit him
to make her happy. And when in due time he
received his eight-day leave, he lashed a couple
of bags to his fighting-plane and literally flew
to her.

There had been a lull in the fighting and her
time was pretty much her own. They made a
number of excursions on foot to points of historic
interest, fished in the canal, and refreshed themselves for the hard work that was still before them.

Sometimes they spoke of Ellen; but tranquilly
and not as of a cherished child who was lost to
them forever. Death no longer seemed a horror
to them, but a natural experience like birth, and
one to be neither more dreaded nor less. Also
they spoke at times, and with perfect naturalness,
of Dayton's other daughter, and on the last day

His Daughter

of his leave Dayton spoke of Claire D'Avril herself.

"Do you ever hear from that nurse—what did she call herself—who was here when I was sick?"

"My roommate—Adèle Soubisse?"

He nodded.

"Often," said Dorothy, "and she always asks after you. I think she's about the happiest woman I know. When the war began, she was with a young doctor, and through him she got a chance to try her hand at hospital work; and because she had the right kind of disposition and was strong as a horse she made good. Every night when we'd had a bad day she used to laugh and say: 'Madame, I am a better woman than I was this morning. How long will it be before I am a good woman like you?' This war proves one thing: that no matter how bad people have been there's hope for them."

"Do you really believe that?"

"Of course I do."

"But there's no undoing what we've done. Take me, for instance."

"We can't undo what we've done, of course," said Dorothy, and she laughed.

"But if you like I will take you—for instance: compared to what you've done since the war began everything else seems to me so little and insignificant that so far as I'm concerned it simply doesn't exist. . . . So far as I'm concerned the past is simply dead and buried; and that is not an act of will-power, it's just a fact. . . . I'm not afraid of the future . . . not one little bit."

He slid an arm around her and laid his cheek against hers.

"There's nothing much that I can say," he said. "I've been bad and I'm trying to be good. . . . Since Ellen died I have done nothing, thought nothing, that could ever hurt you. . . . And so it sort of looks as if there was some good in me. . . . And this time, dear, I won't go weather-vaning with every pretty breeze that blows. . . . I'll stick. I *know* I'll stick!"

They kissed each other lovingly.

"Promise you'll be very careful and not take unnecessary risks."

"Sure," said Dayton.

The next day there existed for him nothing but the enemy against whose wits he had matched his wits and against whose life he had staked his own.

"I got him finally," he wrote to his wife, "but he fell inside his own lines and so didn't count."

www.ingramcontent.com/pod-product-compliance
Lightning Source LLC
Chambersburg PA
CBHW022210010726
47493CB00002B/496